Olivia Harper

And The Witches Of Ravenswood

James Paul Ward

Kindle Direct Publishing

Contents

Contents

Preface

In the hallowed depths of time, where the realms of magic and reality intertwine, a tale of darkness and destiny unfolded. Centuries ago, in the mystical land of Ravenswood, a curse was cast—a curse that would bind the fate of the town and its inhabitants for generations to come.

It was an age of ancient sorcery, when witches roamed the land and their powers soared through the night sky. Among them was a coven known as the Shadowsong Witches, revered for their mastery of the arcane arts. Led by the enigmatic High Priestess Seraphina, they possessed a potent magic that whispered of both light and darkness.

Yet, beneath the facade of harmony and unity, a tempest brewed within Seraphina's heart. Hidden beneath her regal exterior lay a wellspring of resentment, an ancient grudge that smoldered with a searing intensity. The Shadowsong Witches had not always lived in peace.

Deep within the annals of Ravenswood's history, a tragic betrayal had stained their bloodline. Seraphina, once a beacon of compassion and wisdom, had been wronged by her own kin. They had conspired against her, undermining her authority and casting her aside, stripping her of her rightful place as High Priestess.

In the wake of this betrayal, a consuming anger consumed Seraphina. Her heart seethed with a desire for vengeance, and her mind fixated on the notion of power beyond imagination—a power that would make her the undoubted ruler of Ravenswood and its inhabitants.

Blinded by her thirst for dominance, Seraphina turned to the forbidden depths of black magic. She sought power that would surpass anything her fellow witches could fathom, a power that would ensure her supremacy and strike fear into the hearts of those who had wronged her.

Under the pale light of the blood moon, Seraphina's coven gathered in the sacred grove. In a ritual of unspeakable power, fueled by her wrath and driven by her desire for control, she wove a malevolent spell that would forever alter the course of Ravenswood's history.

With each incantation, the earth trembled, and the air crackled with a tangible force. Seraphina's eyes burned with an unholy fire as she invoked the curse upon her own bloodline—a curse that would bind them to eternal torment and unexplainable Comas.

As the final words echoed through the night, a shroud of darkness descended upon the town, its tendrils infiltrating every nook and cranny. The curse took hold, its insidious grip reaching deep into the souls of the witches and their descendants, marking them with an indelible stain.

From that fateful night, the Shadowsong Coven withered into obscurity, their name forgotten by all but the winds of time. Yet, the legacy of their curse endured, casting a pall over the once-thriving community of Ravenswood.

Now, as the sun sets on another era, a new chapter begins—a chapter that holds the key to unraveling the ancient curse. As destiny weaves its intricate tapestry, a spirited teenager named Olivia Harper, descendant of the Shadowsong bloodline, steps into the spotlight. Guided by the whispers of her ancestors and fueled by a determination to break the chains that bind her family, she embarks on a perilous journey alongside her parents, Richard and Emily.

Together, they will delve into the forgotten corners of Ravenswood's history, uncovering forgotten relics, untangling the web of magic, and facing the forces that conspire to keep the curse alive. They will confront their deepest fears, form unlikely alliances, and harness the power of love, for it is in their hands that the fate of Ravenswood and their own bloodline rests.

Chapter One

Awakening to a New Reality

The sun cast its golden glow over the quaint city of Ravenswood, illuminating the picturesque Victorian houses that lined the cobblestone streets. Among them stood the Harper residence, an enchanting abode that seemed frozen in time. Its weathered gray facade boasted intricate wooden carvings and stained glass windows, imbuing the house with an air of mystery and charm.

Inside the Harper home, the aroma of freshly baked cinnamon rolls wafted through the air, embracing the cozy kitchen with a warm embrace. Olivia Harper, a spirited teenager with a mane of chestnut curls, sat at the kitchen table, engrossed in a book. Her parents, Richard and Emily, both creative souls, were artists who found solace in the strokes of their paintbrushes.

"Oh my gosh, this is terrible! So many people just falling into comas out of nowhere," Olivia exclaimed, looking up from her book, concern etched on her face.

"I know, Livvy. It's, like, totally alarming. And it's making me think about the curse that has haunted our family for, like, forever," Emily responded softly, her hair tied in a loose bun.

Richard nodded in agreement. "Yeah, it's not just us anymore. The curse is spreading, and we can't just ignore it. We have to do something."

A spark of determination ignited in Olivia's eyes. "I have a feeling there's more to this curse than we think. Like, I was reading this book earlier, and it mentioned an attic with all these family secrets. Maybe we'll find something there that will help us understand the curse and its connection to Ravenswood."

Emily's excitement grew. "You're, like, totally onto something, Livvy. Let's go up to the attic and see what we can uncover. It's time to confront this curse head-on."

The trio made their way up the creaky staircase, the old wooden steps echoing with each footfall. The attic door stood before them, covered in a thin layer of cobwebs, as if guarding the secrets that lay beyond.

Richard reached for the doorknob and turned it, the door groaning open. A beam of sunlight filtered through the crack, revealing a world untouched by time. Dust particles danced in the sun's rays, giving the attic an ethereal glow.

"Whoa, this is, like, stepping into a forgotten era or something," Olivia whispered in awe as they stepped into the attic.

The space was filled with an eclectic assortment of furniture, trunks, and forgotten artifacts, their outlines veiled in a hazy nostalgia. Each item seemed to hold a whisper of the past, beckoning Olivia to uncover their stories.

Emily's voice carried a touch of wonder as she surveyed the attic. "Oh, the tales these treasures could tell. It's like stepping into a forgotten era."

Richard nodded, his eyes twinkling with anticipation. "Let's not waste another moment. The attic holds the key to our family's past, and who knows what mysteries we'll unravel."

Olivia's heart swelled with excitement. This was more than just a simple exploration of dusty old belongings; it was a journey into their heritage, a chance to discover the hidden chapters of their family's story. Together, they would unearth the secrets that lay dormant, and perhaps, in the process, stumble upon the key to breaking the ancient curse that had befallen their ancestors.

With each step into the attic's embrace, Olivia's curiosity grew stronger, and the whispers of the past echoed through her mind. Little did she know that the attic held not only forgotten treasures but also the gateway to an extraordinary adventure that would forever change their lives.

As Olivia's gaze swept across the attic's hidden treasures, her eyes fell upon a dusty, leather-bound book nestled amidst a pile of aged papers. It seemed to emit a faint shimmer, beckoning her closer. With trembling hands, she reached for the book, its weathered cover yielding to her touch.

A sense of familiarity washed over Olivia as she traced her fingers over the embossed symbols adorning the book. The weight of her family's connection to the cursed witches resurfaced in her mind, and she realized that this discovery was no mere coincidence.

"Mum, Dad," Olivia called out, her voice

quivering with a mixture of excitement and trepidation, "Look what I've found! It's a book, and I think it's connected to the witches we read about."

Emily and Richard rushed to Olivia's side, their eyes widening in astonishment as they recognized the book. "The Chronicles of Ravenswood," Emily whispered, her voice filled with awe. "Could this be the key to unraveling the mysteries that shroud our family's past?"

Richard's brow furrowed with curiosity as he leafed through the aged pages. "It appears to contain the tales and secrets of the cursed witches. If our family truly shares a connection, then this book may hold the answers we've been seeking."

Olivia's heart raced with anticipation as her parents gathered around her, their shared determination igniting a newfound sense of purpose. They delved into the book, immersing themselves in the stories of a bygone era, where magic and curses intertwined.

Page after page, Olivia discovered the tales of the powerful witches who had once graced the land of Ravenswood. Her heart swelled with pride and a tingling sense of responsibility. She realized that the blood of these witches flowed through her veins, and with it came the potential to break the curse that had haunted her ancestors for centuries.

"This is incredible," Olivia whispered, her voice filled with awe and wonder. "We are part of something bigger than ourselves. We have the chance to rewrite our family's history, to free them from the curse that has plagued them for far too long."

Richard and Emily exchanged a knowing glance, their eyes brimming with a mixture of concern and hope. "Olivia," Richard said gently, "we must approach this with caution. The path ahead is riddled with challenges and unknown dangers. But if we stand together as a family, guided by love and a steadfast belief in the power of goodness, we can overcome anything."

Emily placed a comforting hand on Olivia's shoulder, her voice filled with unwavering support. "We will stand by your side, dear. Together, we will face this journey head-on, not only for the sake of our family but also for the town of Ravenswood."

Olivia felt a surge of determination coursing through her veins. She knew that embarking on this perilous journey would test their strength, resilience, and the bonds that held them together. But she also knew that they were destined to break the chains of the old witch's curse, bringing light and redemption to their family and their beloved Ravenswood.

Armed with the ancient knowledge within the Chronicles of Ravenswood, Olivia and her family prepared to uncover the truths that lay hidden beneath layers of time. Little did they know that their search for answers would lead them on a transformative quest, where magic, courage, and the power of love would collide in a battle against the shadows of the past. The stage was set, and the destiny of the Harper family intertwined with the long-lost witches of Ravenswood, ready to rewrite their intertwined fates and forge a future free from the shackles of a centuries-old curse.

With their hearts aflame with determination, Olivia and her family concluded their exploration of the attic, clutching the Chronicles of Ravenswood close to their chests. The weight of their newfound knowledge pressed upon them, a responsibility that could not be ignored. They understood that the fate of their family and the future of Ravenswood now rested on their shoulders.

As they descended the creaky attic stairs, Olivia's mind buzzed with a whirlwind of thoughts and emotions. She knew that breaking the curse would not be an easy task. It would require unraveling ancient spells, unearthing forgotten relics, and confronting powerful forces that had plagued their ancestors for centuries. Yet, in the depths of her being, Olivia felt a glimmer of hope—a belief that love, courage, and unwavering determination could triumph over the darkest of magic.

Gathered in the warm glow of the living room, Olivia, Richard, and Emily sat together, the air thick with anticipation. The Chronicles of Ravenswood lay open on the coffee table, its pages filled with tales of witches, their trials, and the looming threat that hung over their beloved town.

Olivia's voice quivered with resolve as she addressed her parents. "We cannot turn a blind eye to this curse, to the imminent doom that awaits us all. We must act, for the sake of our family and the people of Ravenswood."

Richard nodded, his eyes shining with pride. "You speak the truth, Olivia. We hold the key to saving not only ourselves but also our town. We must embrace our heritage, harness the power that flows through our veins, and break the chains of this ancient curse."

Emily reached out and clasped Olivia's hand, her voice filled with unwavering support. "We are a family, united in love and purpose. Together, we will face the trials that lie ahead, and with each step we take, we will bring hope and salvation to our ancestors and the generations to come."

As the final rays of sunlight bathed the room, Olivia closed her eyes, her mind filled with visions of the challenges that awaited them. She knew that the path they had chosen would test their bonds, push them to their limits, and demand sacrifices. But in the face of adversity, they would stand tall, armed with the strength of their love, the wisdom of their ancestors, and the unwavering belief that good would prevail.

With the echoes of their determination resonating through the room, Olivia and her family poised on the precipice of an extraordinary journey. The first steps had been taken, and the quest to break the ancient curse had begun. Ravenswood and its inhabitants awaited their saviors, unaware of the peril that loomed but destined to witness a tale of bravery, magic, and the indomitable spirit of a young girl named Olivia.

Chapter Two

Whispers Of The Past

Restless sleep evaded Olivia that night, her mind buzzing with the weight of their newfound knowledge and the urgent need to break the curse. Tossing and turning in her bed, she couldn't ignore the constant pull dragging her back to the attic. The forgotten secrets and the desperate hunger for answers invaded her dreams, pushing her to take action.

Unable to resist any longer, Olivia slipped out of her bedroom under the cover of darkness, making sure not to disturb her sleeping parents. The old wooden stairs creaked softly beneath her careful steps as she climbed up to the attic, guided by the moonlight seeping through the attic window.

The attic hung in stillness, filled with anticipation, as if it sensed the momentous discovery about to unravel. Olivia's heart raced as her eyes landed on the vast collection of forgotten treasures. A corner of the room beckoned her, an uncharted territory waiting to be explored.

With each step she took, the floorboards whispered ancient secrets, pulling her closer to the concealed knowledge that awaited her. As Olivia reached the corner, a beam of moonlight revealed a hidden compartment tucked within an intricately carved armoire.

Her hands trembled as she cautiously opened the compartment, revealing a broomstick hidden beneath layers of time. It exuded an otherworldly energy, pulsating with untapped potential. Olivia's breath caught in her throat as she recognized it as her ancestor's broomstick, the one who had been cursed alongside the others.

She lifted the broomstick delicately, awestruck by its craftsmanship and the mysteries it held. She could almost hear her ancestor's whispers, urging her to embrace her heritage and unleash the magic within.

A surge of anticipation surged through Olivia's

veins as she straddled the broomstick, her fingertips tingling with newfound energy. In that moment, she felt an indescribable connection to her ancestor, a lineage of powerful witches waiting to be unleashed. The broomstick responded to her touch, vibrating with dormant power, as if it yearned to aid her in the battle against the curse.

Olivia's mind buzzed with questions and possibilities. How could this broomstick assist them in breaking the curse? What secrets were concealed within its ancient wood? With each passing moment, her determination solidified, and a fire ignited within her, fueled by her resolve to protect her family and the town of Ravenswood.

As she descended from the attic, clutching the broomstick tightly, Olivia's heart brimmed with hope. This discovery marked a turning point in their journey, a tangible symbol of their magical lineage. With the broomstick by their side, they would soar through the skies, confronting the darkest depths of their history and forging a path towards redemption.

Dawn painted the horizon with a golden hue as Olivia returned to her room, carefully concealing the broomstick beneath her bed. Finally, sleep embraced her, dreams swirling with visions of ancient spells, daring adventures, and the triumph that awaited them.

The broomstick, a silent witness to the whispers of the past, would become their powerful tool in the fight against the curse. Ravenswood remained unaware of the magical forces stirring within its very own guardian witch.

The following morning, sunlight streamed through the windows of the cozy kitchen as Olivia sat at the breakfast table with her parents. The aroma of freshly brewed coffee and warm pastries filled the air, momentarily easing the weight of their impending quest.

Richard and Emily exchanged gentle smiles, their eyes filled with a mix of pride and concern for their daughter. It was clear that their thoughts were consumed by the same burning desire to break the curse that had haunted their family for generations.

As they finished breakfast, Olivia's gaze drifted towards the staircase, momentarily distracted by the broomstick's presence hidden beneath her bed. Its mystery tugged at her once again, beckoning her to explore the depths of its power and uncover the secrets it held.

"Hey, guys," Olivia began, her voice filled with curiosity and excitement. "I just remembered something I left upstairs. Mind if I go grab it real quick?"

Richard and Emily exchanged knowing glances, understanding Olivia's insatiable thirst for knowledge. They nodded in unison, giving her permission to venture back upstairs.

As Olivia hurried up the stairs, her mind raced with anticipation. She reached her room and retrieved the broomstick, cradling it in her hands. Its sleek design felt familiar, as if it belonged in the modern era just as much as it did in the realm of ancient magic. Her eyes fell upon the engraved markings on the handle, and she noticed the faint glow they emitted.

In a hushed voice, Olivia recited the enchanting words inscribed on the broomstick, her voice filled with a mix of reverence and determination. "Ignis ascendere. Potentia eligere." The phrases rolled off her tongue, carrying the weight of centuries-old incantations.

Suddenly, the broomstick hummed with electric energy, its dormant magic awakening in response to Olivia's invocation. Vibrant sparks of light danced along its length, casting a mesmerizing glow, while a gentle breeze enveloped the room. Olivia's eyes widened in awe as the broomstick came to life, levitating just above her open palm.

Richard and Emily, alerted by the shift in

energy, rushed into Olivia's room, their eyes widening with astonishment as they witnessed the broomstick's enchanting display.

"Olivia!" Richard exclaimed, his voice tinged with disbelief. "You've unlocked its power! The broomstick has chosen you as its rightful wielder."

Emily's hand flew to her mouth, her eyes shimmering with a mix of pride and wonder. "It seems fate has placed this ancient artifact in your hands, my dear. You're meant to harness its magic and lead us toward freedom."

Olivia's heart pounded with exhilaration as she firmly grasped the broomstick, feeling its pulsating energy course through her veins. She had become the chosen one, a modern-day heir to a lineage of witches, entrusted with the responsibility of breaking the curse. The weight of her destiny settled upon her shoulders, but she stood tall, ready to embrace the challenge.

With newfound confidence, Olivia mounted the broomstick, her grip steady and determined. The room buzzed with anticipation as the broomstick responded to her touch, lifting her into the air with graceful ease. She hovered above the ground, her excitement mingling with the sense of liberation and empowerment that filled her.

Her parents watched in awe, their faces illuminated by the radiant light emanating from their daughter and her newfound magical companion. They knew that their journey had taken an unexpected turn, but in that moment, they also understood that Olivia possessed the power to shatter the curse and set their family free.

With her heart brimming with excitement, Olivia couldn't resist the allure of the broomstick's power. She longed to explore its capabilities and forge a deeper connection with her magical ally. Hovering in her bedroom, she made up her mind. She wanted to take the broomstick for a ride, to venture beyond the confines of her room and into the vastness of the world.

"Hey, Dad," Olivia called out, her voice brimming with eagerness. "Mind opening the window for me? I'm about to embark on a little adventure."

Richard, still captivated by the wonders before him, hurried to comply. He swung open the bedroom window, allowing the refreshing morning breeze to sweep into the room, intertwining with the mystical energy that enveloped Olivia and the broomstick.

Olivia's eyes sparkled with anticipation as she maneuvered the broomstick towards the window.

With a swift motion, she soared out into the open air, her hair billowing behind her. The world expanded before her, revealing a panoramic view of the picturesque town of Ravenswood.

However, as Olivia was still getting the hang of riding the broomstick, she encountered an unexpected obstacle—a flock of birds swooping across her path. Startled, she veered to avoid them but misjudged her maneuver and flew right through the flock. Feathers went flying in every direction as the birds squawked and scattered, their comical reaction adding a touch of chaos to Olivia's airborne adventure.

Amidst the flurry of feathers, Olivia let out a surprised yelp, her hair now adorned with a few stray feathers. The broomstick wobbled momentarily, but she managed to regain her balance, laughing at the unexpected encounter. The birds, now regrouping and chirping indignantly, watched as she continued her flight, their presence a comical reminder of the unpredictability of her newfound abilities.

As the morning sun cast its golden rays upon Olivia, she reveled in the sheer joy of flight. She dipped and swerved, her laughter mingling with the wind, echoing through the city below. The broomstick's magic coursed through her veins, and she felt a profound sense of belonging, as if she had found her true place in the world.

After a brilliant morning adventure, Olivia guided the broomstick back towards her bedroom window, descending gracefully to solid ground. Her feet touched the floor, but her spirit still soared. She burst into her parents' presence, her eyes shining with exhilaration and a smile stretching across her face.

"Mother, Father," she exclaimed, barely able to contain her excitement, "you won't believe what I've just experienced! Flying on the broomstick was beyond anything I could have imagined. And guess what? I had a little mishap with a flock of birds! Feathers were flying everywhere, and I'm pretty sure I had a couple in my hair!"

Richard and Emily couldn't help but laugh, their amusement mingling with their pride. They could picture the scene, feathers fluttering in the air as Olivia navigated her way through the unexpected challenge.

Emily chuckled, "Oh, dear! I'm glad you managed to fly through it all unscathed. It seems even the birds couldn't resist a little adventure with you!"

Richard joined in the laughter, adding, "You certainly know how to make an entrance,

Olivia! Feathers and all! Your adventures on that broomstick are bound to be unforgettable."

Chapter Three

Secrets and Friendships

Olivia's heart was still abuzz from her exhilarating broomstick ride. But time was not on her side. She barely had a moment to catch her breath before the inevitable call of education beckoned—school awaited, with its mundane routines and ordinary classrooms.

She hastily gathered her books and bid farewell to her parents, a twinkle of mischief lingering in her eyes. Olivia knew that beneath the façade of a typical teenager, a world of magic simmered, waiting to be unveiled. But until now, she'd had to tread carefully, keeping her secret close to her heart.

As she arrived at school, the bustling halls

filled with students served as a stark contrast to the enchantment that had embraced her that morning. Amidst the throng, Olivia spotted her two closest friends, Sophia and Benjamin, waiting by the lockers.

Sophia stood out in a crowd with her vibrant red curls cascading down her back, accentuating her fair complexion. Her emerald green eyes sparkled with mischief, mirroring Olivia's spirit. She had an infectious laugh that could light up even the dullest moments. Sophia's fashion sense was as eclectic as her personality, often clad in bohemian-inspired clothing that perfectly reflected her free-spirited nature.

Beside her, Benjamin exuded a calm and composed demeanor. His sandy brown hair was neatly styled, and his hazel eyes held a warm, friendly gaze. Benjamin possessed a quiet intelligence, his analytical mind always seeking to understand the world around him. With a penchant for classic literature and a penchant for vintage fashion, Benjamin exuded a timeless charm that set him apart.

As Olivia approached her friends, she greeted them with a warm smile. "Hey, guys! Ready for another day of adventures?" She rolled her eyes.

Sophia smirked sarcastically. "Absolutely! Who

knows what surprises await us today?"

Benjamin nodded, a hint of curiosity in his eyes. "Indeed, Olivia. Life is full of mysteries just waiting to be unraveled."

Together, they walked through the school halls, sharing stories and exchanging laughs. Olivia cherished their friendship, the bond they shared, but the weight of her hidden powers pressed upon her shoulders.

As the trio reached their respective classrooms, they bid each other farewell, their friendship temporarily on hold until the next break. Olivia watched them disappear into the crowd, her heart heavy with unspoken truths.

As the school day progressed, Olivia's mind couldn't escape the weight of the curse that plagued her family, casting a shadow over her thoughts. The conversations she overheard between her parents during restless nights echoed in her mind. The curse was growing stronger, more dangerous, and it extended beyond her family, threatening the safety of the entire community. Something was fueling its power, and Olivia couldn't shake off the urgency to find a solution.

Math class became a blur, equations and formulas blending together as her thoughts consumed her. She glanced at Sophia and Benjamin seated nearby, their faces a comforting presence amidst her swirling worries. They were her allies, her confidants, and she needed their help now more than ever.

As the final bell rang, marking the end of the school day, Olivia gathered her courage. It was time to reveal her secret, to invite Sophia and Benjamin into her magical world. She knew it wouldn't be easy, but their friendship had proven resilient. If anyone could understand and assist her, it would be them.

With determination in her heart, Olivia approached her friends. "Hey, Sophia, Benjamin. I was wondering if you both could come over to my place this afternoon. There's something important I need to share with you."

Sophia's eyes widened with curiosity. "Of course, Liv! We'll be there. Is everything alright?"

Olivia mustered a smile, hoping to reassure them despite the gravity of the situation. "I'll explain everything when you arrive. Just know that it's something... extraordinary."

Benjamin's analytical gaze held a mix of concern and intrigue. "We'll be there to support you, Olivia. You know you can count on us."

With the promise of their unwavering support, Olivia's burden lightened ever so slightly. She had taken the first step toward breaking the barriers of secrecy and forging a stronger bond with her friends. As she headed home, her mind filled with possibilities and the hope that Sophia and Benjamin could help uncover the answers she desperately sought.

The afternoon sun cast a warm glow as Sophia and Benjamin arrived at Olivia's house, curiosity etched on their faces. Olivia greeted them at the door, the broomstick clutched tightly in her hand, an enigmatic smile playing on her lips. Their eyes flickered with confusion, questioning the presence of the broomstick.

Sophia's brow furrowed. "Olivia, why are you holding a broomstick? Is this some kind of joke?"

Olivia's voice carried a mix of reassurance and excitement. "I promise, it's not a joke. I'll explain everything, but we need to go on a little journey first."

With a sense of trepidation and curiosity, Sophia and Benjamin followed Olivia as she led them through the woods. The path meandered through a part of the grounds they had never explored before, their anticipation mounting with each step. After what felt like an eternity, they reached the end of the path, where a rundown cottage stood in solemn silence.

Olivia turned to her friends, her eyes sparkling with determination. "This place holds the truth. Inside this cottage, you'll find artifacts and knowledge that pertain to our family's legacy—witchcraft."

Sophia and Benjamin exchanged bewildered glances, their minds struggling to comprehend the revelation. Benjamin, ever the skeptic, spoke up. "Olivia, this is a lot to take in. I need some kind of proof. I can't simply believe without evidence."

A fire ignited in Olivia's eyes, a determination to unveil her true self. She led Benjamin and Sophia into the cottage, where shelves lined with ancient tomes and mystical artifacts greeted their eyes. The air carried a mysterious energy, as if the very essence of magic lingered within those dilapidated walls.

With a deep breath, Olivia began her tale, weaving the intricate history of her lineage. Her words painted a tapestry of powerful witches, ancestral curses, and the impending danger that plagued their family and the town itself. She spoke of her unwavering belief in their shared abilities, the legacy they carried.

But Benjamin's analytical mind yearned for tangible proof, a testament to shatter his doubts. With Olivia's guidance, they stepped outside the cottage, the cool breeze whispering secrets in their ears. Olivia mounted the broomstick, her heart pounding with anticipation. She cast a glance at Sophia and Benjamin, their eyes wide with wonder.

In a single, fluid motion, Olivia leaped into the air, the broomstick lifting her gently off the ground. She soared gracefully above the cottage, defying gravity itself. Sophia and Benjamin watched, their disbelief transforming into awe as they witnessed their friend embracing her birthright.

The moment suspended in time, their hearts entwined with magic, Sophia and Benjamin saw a truth that shattered their skepticism. A newfound realization dawned upon them—Olivia was not just an ordinary girl. She was a witch, and the extraordinary powers she possessed unfolded before their eyes.

Olivia gracefully descended from her airborne journey, landing on solid ground with a sense of purpose. Benjamin, his disbelief slowly dissipating, stared at Olivia with wide eyes. "You're a witch?" he uttered, his voice filled with astonishment and a hint of wonder.

Sophia, her intuition guiding her, nodded in agreement. "I've always sensed there was something different about you, Olivia. Now it all makes sense."

Olivia took a deep breath, her gaze steady as she looked into the eyes of her friends. "Thanks guys for believing in me. But now, I need your help more than ever. You see, the curse that plagues my family is causing unimaginable suffering. It randomly selects members of our family, causing them to fall into comas without any explanation or warning."

She paused, gathering her thoughts before continuing, her voice filled with urgency and determination. "The curse was confined to our family for generations, but now it has seeped into our community, affecting random people from the town as well. It's growing stronger, and there's something fueling its power, something dark and sinister."

Olivia's voice trembled with a mix of sadness and determination as she continued, "Centuries ago, a sorceress, driven by envy and vengefulness, cast this curse upon my ancestors. Its purpose was to strip away their powers and bring suffering. It was meant to fade over time, but instead, it has grown stronger, beyond what was ever intended."

She met their eyes, her expression earnest. "My parents have been discussing the curse's progression, the signs of its deepening hold. We need to find out what is amplifying its malevolence, what external force is feeding its strength beyond its original purpose."

Olivia took a step closer to Sophia and Benjamin, her voice filled with both desperation and determination. "We cannot let this curse consume our town, our loved ones. We must uncover the source, the external force that's empowering it beyond its limits. And I need your help."

Benjamin, his analytical mind now fully engaged, absorbed the information, piecing together the fragments of their shared reality. He nodded solemnly. "Olivia, Sophia, I may have had doubts before, but now I see the truth before my eyes. We can't just watch as this curse takes over our community. We'll do whatever it takes to help you and your family break it once and for all."

Sophia's unwavering loyalty shone in her eyes as she interlaced her fingers with Olivia's. "You're not alone in this, Olivia. We'll stand by your side, facing whatever challenges come our way. Together, we will confront this curse and restore peace to our community."

A sense of unity enveloped them, their bond strengthened by their shared determination. The weight of their responsibility lay heavy on their shoulders, but hope bloomed amidst the darkness. Olivia knew that with Sophia and Benjamin by her side, they had a fighting chance to unravel the mysteries, confront the growing evil, and ultimately break the curse that threatened their world.

Chapter 5 marked the beginning of their journey, a journey fueled by friendship, belief, and the unwavering spirit to protect their loved ones. The path ahead was treacherous, but they would face it united, wielding their newfound knowledge and determination against the encroaching curse.

As Olivia, Sophia, and Benjamin stood united, committed to their mission, a soft rustling of leaves caught their attention. Turning toward the sound, they saw Olivia's parents, Richard and Emily, emerge from the shadows, their presence commanding attention like never before.

Richard, a tall and dignified figure with a salt-and-pepper beard, wore a deep blue robe adorned with intricate silver patterns that shimmered under the dappled sunlight. Emily, a graceful and gentle woman with flowing auburn hair, donned a flowing emerald green robe, embroidered with delicate vines that seemed to come to life as she moved.

Olivia stepped forward, her voice filled with a mix of nervousness and excitement. "Mom, Dad, I've told them about our family secret, they want to help us break the curse."

Richard and Emily exchanged a knowing glance, their eyes filled with gratitude and understanding. Richard spoke first, his voice carrying a sense of sincerity. "Hey Sophia, hey Benjamin. We're glad you're here and that Olivia has trusted you with our family secret. Today, you get a glimpse of our true selves, embracing the magic within us."

Emily's warm smile embraced the newcomers. "Absolutely. You've seen us in our everyday clothes, but today we wanted to show you a different side of us. We appreciate your support and willingness to stand by Olivia. Together, we'll find a way to break the curse."

Sophia, still processing the unexpected revelation, found her voice. "Mr. and Mrs. Harper, it's really cool to meet you like this. Olivia has told us some about your family's heritage, but seeing it firsthand is pretty incredible. We're here for whatever it takes to break the curse and protect everyone we care about."

Benjamin, his analytical mind searching for understanding, added, "The power and knowledge that you possess are fascinating. We're honored to be part of this journey and contribute our skills to help. Let's face the challenges together."

Richard placed a reassuring hand on Benjamin's

shoulder. "Your logical thinking will definitely come in handy, Benjamin. We appreciate your insights and unique perspective. We're glad to have you on our team."

Olivia's parents shared a nod, their eyes filled with pride and appreciation. Emily spoke with a comforting tone. "Thank you, Sophia and Benjamin, for trusting us and joining Olivia's mission. Together, we'll navigate the obstacles that lie ahead, drawing strength from our unity and shared purpose."

As the group stood within the cottage, a sense of purpose filled the air. Sophia and Benjamin realized they were part of something bigger, entrusted with a mission that held the well-being of their loved ones and their community. Olivia's parents, dressed casually yet radiating a sense of wisdom, stood as mentors, ready to guide them through the challenges ahead.

Chapter Four

Moonlit Spells

In the heart of the Harper household, the kitchen exuded a cozy warmth that enveloped the room. Soft rays of sunlight filtered through the curtains, casting a gentle glow on the teenagers huddled around the sturdy oak table. Ancient tomes, weathered scrolls, and the Chronicles of Ravenswood sprawled across the worn surface, as if whispering secrets of old.

Olivia, determined to unlock the secrets of the ancient spells, had dedicated herself to studying day and night. She delved into the pages of dusty tomes, her fingers tracing the faded text with reverence. With each passing day, her understanding of the mystical arts deepened, and she grew more confident in her abilities.

Sophia and Benjamin, though not blessed with magical abilities, were unwavering in their support for Olivia. They diligently researched any historical records or legends that could offer clues to breaking the curse. Benjamin's analytical mind proved invaluable in deciphering riddles and interpreting cryptic texts, while Sophia's intuition guided them toward unexpected solutions.

During one particularly intense study session, Olivia became visibly overwhelmed by the complexity of the spells. She buried her face in her hands, her voice tinged with frustration. "I feel like I'm missing something crucial. If only there were more hints in these ancient texts."

Sophia reached out, placing a reassuring hand on Olivia's shoulder. "Hey, Liv, don't stress too much. Remember, even Gandalf needed a cheat sheet for his spells sometimes."

Benjamin chuckled, joining in the lighthearted banter. "Yeah, I bet he had a secret pocket in his robe filled with 'Wizard for Dummies' books."

Olivia couldn't help but smile at their attempts to lighten the mood. "Well, if Gandalf had a cheat sheet, maybe we should create our own magical Cliff Notes version."

Sophia playfully wagged her finger. "But only if it's ethically sourced from ancient wizards who willingly shared their knowledge."

The trio shared a laugh, momentarily easing the weight of their quest. They knew the road ahead wouldn't be easy, but they were determined to face it together, even if it meant adding a dash of humor to their magical endeavors.

One evening, as they took a break from their intensive training, Sophia suggested a well-deserved escape into the world of modern entertainment. "Hey, guys," she said, a mischievous twinkle in her eyes, "we've been working so hard. How about we go to the town's cinema and catch a movie? A little break might give our minds a chance to recharge."

Olivia and Benjamin exchanged glances, their tired faces lighting up with excitement. Olivia nodded eagerly. "That sounds like a fantastic idea, Sophia! A movie sounds like the perfect way to unwind for a bit."

The trio set out into town, their steps light and their spirits lifted. They immersed themselves in the cinematic world, discussing the options for their movie night as they walked. As they reached the theater, the vibrant marquee displayed a variety of choices, each promising an escape from reality.

"Hmm, what do you guys feel like watching?" Benjamin asked, scanning the movie titles. "There's a fantasy adventure film called 'Mystic Quest,' a sci-fi thriller called 'Quantum Shift,' and a heartwarming coming-of-age story called 'Whispering Dreams.'"

Sophia's eyes sparkled with excitement. "I vote for 'Mystic Quest'! It's all about magical realms and epic quests. It might give us some inspiration too!"

Olivia grinned, nodding in agreement. "Sounds perfect! Let's step into a world of magic and adventure for a while."

The trio purchased their tickets, the anticipation bubbling within them. As they settled into their seats, the theater's dim lights and the smell of freshly buttered popcorn created an atmosphere of cinematic delight.

Throughout the movie, Sophia and Benjamin exchanged knowing glances during particularly thrilling moments. Benjamin's cheeks would color ever so slightly, and Sophia couldn't help but giggle softly. The magic on the screen seemed to reflect the blossoming connection between them, adding an unexpected charm to their movie night.

After the credits rolled, they stepped out of the theater, their hearts still racing from the exhilarating tale they had witnessed. The night air felt cooler against their faces, but their spirits burned with a renewed sense of determination.

"I never thought I'd say this, but that movie made me want to pick up a sword and go on a quest," Benjamin joked, a playful smirk on his face.

Sophia chuckled, nudging his arm. "Well, I'm always here to be your trusty sidekick if you ever need one, Sir Benjamin!"

Olivia grinned, wrapping her arm around Sophia's shoulder. "And I'll be right there with you, cheering you both on. But for now, how about we satisfy our earthly appetites? I'm craving some delicious diner food."

Just down the street was a diner that was a local favorite. The teens had eaten there many times after school and they knew the menu well. The trio headed inside the diner, its neon sign buzzing with warmth and the promise of a comforting meal. As they pushed open the door, laughter and chatter greeted them, blending with the enticing aroma of sizzling bacon and freshly brewed coffee.

The diner's menu offered a mouthwatering array of options, from classic burgers and milkshakes to hearty platters of pancakes and eggs. The trio placed their orders, each selecting their favorite comfort food. Olivia couldn't resist the allure of a bacon cheeseburger, while Sophia opted for a stack of fluffy blueberry pancakes. Benjamin, always the adventurous eater, decided on a plate of loaded nachos.

As they waited for their meals to arrive, their conversation flowed effortlessly, the recent movie still fresh in their minds. "Did you see the way the main character used those magic spells?" Sophia said, her eyes sparkling with excitement. "It reminded me of how you control the magical energies, Liv."

Olivia's cheeks flushed with a mixture of pride and bashfulness. "Aw, thanks, Sophia. It's all about focus and channeling your intentions, just like they showed in the movie."

Benjamin, ever the skeptic, couldn't help but chime in with a playful smirk. "But let's not forget the scene where they tried to cast a spell and ended up summoning a chicken instead. I hope that doesn't happen during our actual ritual."

Olivia giggled, nudging him with her elbow. "Oh, come on, Ben. If we accidentally summon a chicken, we'll just have to ask it nicely to leave."

Their laughter filled the air, and for a moment, the weight of their quest lifted. They were just three teenagers enjoying a night out, without the burden of curses and ancient magic.

As their meals arrived, they dug into the delicious food with gusto, savoring each bite. The clinking of cutlery and the occasional satisfied sigh filled the diner booth, creating a warm ambiance that matched the glowing diner sign outside.

In the midst of their feast, Sophia and Benjamin exchanged another knowing glance, their eyes lingering a little longer this time. Olivia noticed the subtle exchange and couldn't help but raise an eyebrow playfully.

"Okay, you two. Spill the beans. What's with all the secret glances?" she teased, a mischievous smile tugging at the corners of her lips.

Sophia blushed, her cheeks turning a shade of pink that matched the strawberry syrup on her pancakes. "Well, um, it's just... Benjamin and I were talking during the movie, and, uh, we realized we might have more in common than we thought."

Benjamin joined in, a coy smile on his face. "Yeah, and, um, I must admit, Sophia's pretty amazing. We make a great team, and, uh, I really enjoy spending time with her."

Olivia's grin widened, and she playfully nudged

Sophia with her elbow. "Well, well, well, it seems like the magic of friendship isn't the only kind of magic in the air tonight."

Sophia playfully rolled her eyes, but there was a hint of delight in her voice. "Oh, stop it, Liv. It's just a hunch for now."

Benjamin chimed in, his confidence growing. "Yeah, just a hunch. But I think it's a pretty good one."

Their lighthearted banter continued as they finished their meal, the air filled with laughter and warmth. As they left the diner, their spirits were high, and they felt ready to take on whatever challenges the future held.

Outside, the moon hung low in the sky, casting a silvery glow over the town. The Blood Moon, the catalyst for their upcoming ritual, loomed closer on the horizon. But for now, the trio relished in the simple joy of being teenagers out for a night of fun and friendship.

As the teens made their way back to Olivia's house, the moonlight cast eerie shadows across the familiar streets of Ravenswood. Laughter and chatter echoed from distant corners, signifying that the town was still alive despite the late hour. But amidst the usual sounds, there was something else –

a faint chanting that seemed to hang in the air like a haunting melody.

Sophia's brow furrowed, her senses on high alert. "Do you guys hear that?" she asked, her voice barely above a whisper.

Olivia strained her ears, trying to make sense of the distant sounds. "Yeah, I hear it too. It's like... chanting? But that can't be right. My family and I are the only ones left of our bloodline in Ravenswood."

Benjamin's mind kicked in, his gaze scanning the darkened streets. "It might be a group of people from the neighboring town or just some late-night revelers. Let's go check it out, just to be sure."

As they ventured closer, the chanting grew louder, and they realized that it was coming from the direction of an old, abandoned mansion at the edge of town. The mansion had long been rumored to be haunted, and no one dared to go near it after sunset.

Olivia's heart pounded in her chest as she gripped her friends' hands tightly. "Guys, I don't have a good feeling about this."

As they reached the mansion's rusty iron gates, they peered through the cracks, trying to catch a glimpse of the source of the chanting. Shadows danced within, and an ominous aura surrounded the place.

Sophia's voice trembled slightly as she whispered, "Maybe we should go back. This doesn't feel right."

Benjamin nodded in agreement, but his curiosity was still piqued. "Olivia, are you sure there's no one else from your family in town? Maybe there's a distant relative or something."

Olivia shook her head. "I'm certain. My parents and I are the last of our bloodline. There's no one else here who practices magic."

The chanting intensified, and the teens exchanged nervous glances. Just as they were about to turn back, a sudden gust of wind rattled the gates, making them creak open slightly.

Olivia gasped, her eyes widening with alarm. "That's strange. The gates are usually locked. Someone must be inside."

Sophia's heart pounded in her chest, but her determination kicked in. "We can't leave it to chance. Let's go inside and find out what's going on."

Benjamin hesitated for a moment but then nodded, his sense of duty prevailing. "Okay, but let's stick together and be cautious."

The three friends entered the mansion, their footsteps echoing in the grand entrance hall. Moonlight streamed through broken windows, illuminating the dust-filled air. As they followed the chanting, it led them deeper into the mansion, through winding corridors and up a creaky staircase.

The sound seemed to come from a room at the end of the hallway, where faint flickers of candlelight peeked through the gaps in the doorframe.

Sophia whispered, "I have a bad feeling about this, guys. Maybe we should just call the police."

Olivia, her determination unwavering, shook her head. "We can't involve the police in something like this. They won't understand."

The chanting grew louder, and with every step, their hearts pounded louder in their chests. As they reached the door, their hands trembling, Olivia pushed it open slightly.

The room beyond was bathed in an otherworldly glow, filled with robed figures in the midst of a mysterious ritual. Their voices rose and fell in an ancient language, their movements synchronized and purposeful.

Olivia's eyes widened in shock. "What... what is this? Who are they?"

Before they could process what they were witnessing, a sudden gust of wind slammed the door shut behind them, plunging them into darkness.

Chapter Five

The Coven of Shadows

As the door slammed shut, the room plunged into darkness, leaving Olivia and her friends momentarily disoriented. Their breaths quickened, their hearts pounding in their chests, as they fumbled for their cell phones, desperate for a source of light.

With a soft click, the screens illuminated the room, revealing a scene that sent shivers down their spines. The room was adorned with symbols and sigils etched into the walls, and an altar at the center, adorned with candles that flickered with an otherworldly glow.

Before them stood the coven, their faces hidden

beneath hoods, their presence exuding an aura of malevolence. At their forefront stood a woman with flowing dark hair and piercing eyes, Cassandra, the enigmatic leader of the coven.

Cassandra's voice dripped with a mixture of charm and menace as she addressed the intruders. "Well, well, what do we have here? Young fools stumbling into our sacred sanctuary. How unfortunate for you."

Olivia's voice quivered, but she managed to muster a hint of defiance. "Who are you? What do you want?"

Cassandra's lips curled into a sinister smile. "We are the Coven of Shadows, dear girl, and we have been aware of your quest to break the curse. But I'm afraid we can't allow that. The curse holds immense power, and we intend to use it for our own purposes."

Sophia, her eyes narrowing, stepped forward, her voice laced with determination. "You think you can just take advantage of this curse? You're gravely mistaken. We won't let you succeed."

Cassandra laughed, the sound echoing through the room, sending chills down their spines. "Oh, my dear, you underestimate the power we wield. Your efforts will be in vain. We have prepared for this moment for centuries."

Benjamin, always the voice of reason, interjected, his voice laced with skepticism. "Centuries? You're bluffing. Magic may be real, but your claims are nothing more than delusions of grandeur."

Cassandra's eyes narrowed, her tone growing colder. "You dare question me? You, who possess no magic? You may play a part in this tale, but you are but shadows compared to what we are capable of."

Olivia, her voice filled with determination, stepped forward, her hazel eyes blazing. "We may not have the same powers as you, but we have something you will never understand. Friendship, trust, and the strength to fight against darkness. We won't let you use the curse for evil."

The tension in the room thickened, as if the air itself held its breath. The standoff between Olivia's group and the coven set the stage for the final battle, a clash of wills that would determine the fate of Ravenswood.

Cassandra's chilling laughter echoed once again. "So be it. We shall see who triumphs in the end. But mark my words, young ones, you have no idea of the forces you are up against."

In a sudden and sinister display of power, Cassandra waved her hands, summoning chains that materialized out of thin air. The chains slithered and coiled around Olivia, Sophia, and Benjamin, ensnaring them tightly. The trio's eyes widened in shock and alarm as they found themselves helplessly bound.

Cassandra approached them, a malevolent smile dancing on her lips. "You should feel honored to be part of this momentous occasion," she hissed. "Your bloodline was always meant to serve the curse, and now, as the Blood Moon approached, your sacrifice would ensure its everlasting power."

Olivia struggled against her restraints, her voice tinged with defiance. "You won't get away with this, Cassandra. We'll find a way to stop you and protect Ravenswood."

Sophia, her fiery spirit undeterred, added with a determined glint in her eyes, "You may have trapped us, but our spirits remain unyielding. We'll fight until the very end."

Benjamin, though unable to break free, maintained a steely resolve. "Your treachery won't go unanswered, Cassandra. We'll find a way to thwart your plans and save ourselves."

Cassandra chuckled darkly, her voice dripping

with malice. "Oh, how you underestimate me, dear children. You won't be leaving this place until the time is right. Enjoy your temporary confinement."

With a wave of her hand, one of the coven members stepped forward, following Cassandra's orders. The chains tightened their grip on Olivia, Sophia, and Benjamin, immobilizing them further. The coven member guided the three teens to a dimly lit holding cell in the basement, where they would remain until Cassandra deemed them necessary for her nefarious ritual.

As they were locked away, uncertainty and apprehension filled the air. Olivia's mind raced, desperately searching for a way to escape their captivity and foil Cassandra's plans. Sophia's determination shone through, her eyes gleaming with a hint of rebellion. Benjamin, ever resourceful, mentally analyzed their situation, seeking any weaknesses they could exploit.

Trapped in the dimly lit basement, the air heavy with a musty scent, Olivia, Sophia, and Benjamin found themselves surrounded by cold stone walls that seemed to press in on them. The space was vast, with low ceilings and damp patches spreading across the floor. Flickering fluorescent lights cast eerie shadows, giving the room an unsettling ambiance.

The absence of their cell phones, confiscated by the coven before their imprisonment, left the teens feeling isolated and helpless. The loss of connection to the outside world only heightened their sense of despair. They huddled together in the center of the cramped cell, their spirits dampened by the weight of their circumstances.

Distant sounds of dripping water echoed throughout the basement, creating an eerie symphony of suspense. The occasional scurrying of unseen creatures along the walls added to the atmosphere of uncertainty. The only source of illumination came from a small barred window near the ceiling, through which a sliver of moonlight barely penetrated, serving as a constant reminder of the approaching Blood Moon and their impending doom.

Olivia ran her fingers through her hair, frustration etched on her face. "We're running out of time," she whispered, her voice tinged with desperation. "We need to find a way out of here and stop Cassandra before it's too late."

Sophia leaned against the cold stone wall, her eyes scanning the surroundings. "If only we had our phones," she muttered. "We could contact someone for help."

Benjamin paced back and forth, his mind racing

with thoughts of escape. "There must be a weakness in their hold on us," he mused aloud. "We just need to find it, exploit it, and break free."

As their voices filled the confined space, a mix of determination and uncertainty lingered in the air. The basement seemed to close in on them, heightening their feeling of entrapment. With each passing moment, the urgency to break free and thwart Cassandra's plans intensified, propelling them to search for a glimmer of hope amidst the darkness.

As the hours dragged on, exhaustion began to take its toll on Benjamin and Sophia. Their eyelids grew heavy, and their bodies yearned for rest. Olivia, ever aware of the need to preserve their energy, mustered a small smile despite the dire circumstances.

"We can't let fatigue defeat us," Olivia whispered, her voice filled with determination. "We must find strength in the midst of darkness. Rest, my friends, for tomorrow will bring new challenges, and we need to be ready."

Nodding in agreement, Benjamin and Sophia shuffled closer to Olivia, seeking warmth and solace in their huddled embrace. The coldness of the basement seemed to seep into their bones, but the bond between them provided a comforting respite.

In an attempt to lighten the heavy atmosphere, Sophia mustered a weak smile and playfully nudged Benjamin. "You can sleep next to me, Benjamin, as long as you promise to behave yourself," she teased, hoping to bring a momentary reprieve from their grim reality.

A soft chuckle escaped Benjamin's lips, his eyes reflecting a mixture of amusement and weariness. "I make no promises," he replied, his voice laced with a hint of playfulness, but his energy quickly waning.

With a collective sigh, the three friends succumbed to the exhaustion that had enveloped them. They closed their eyes, finding solace in the closeness of their shared warmth. Sleep, albeit uneasy, provided a temporary escape from their predicament, a chance to gather strength and prepare for the challenges that awaited them in the coming day.

In the dimly lit basement, their rhythmic breaths created a lullaby of resilience, a testament to their unwavering spirit. As they drifted into slumber, uncertainty and hope intertwined in their dreams, paving the way for the battles they would face upon waking.

Chapter Six

The Great Escape

The dawn broke through the small basement window, casting a pale light on the weary faces of Olivia, Sophia, and Benjamin. Their slumber had been restless, interrupted by the cold hardness of their surroundings. However, their respite was abruptly shattered by the arrival of a young girl, a member of the coven.

The girl cautiously approached, her eyes downcast and hands trembling as she carried a tray of meager provisions. The food before them was unappetizing, barely recognizable as nourishment. Despite her fear, a glimmer of kindness flickered in the girl's eyes as she silently placed the tray before them.

Sophia's gaze lingered on the girl, her curiosity piqued by the girl's contrasting demeanor. "Who are you?" Sophia asked in a hushed voice, hoping to engage in a brief conversation.

The girl glanced nervously at the closed door, fear etched across her features. "I-I can't say much," she stammered, her voice barely above a whisper. "But I... I don't want any harm to come to you."

Before Sophia could press further, the girl darted away, her footsteps echoing faintly as she disappeared into the shadows. It was evident that she held secrets, perhaps a spark of defiance against the darkness that engulfed them.

As the door creaked shut, Sophia let out a sigh, her disappointment palpable. "If only we had some means of communication," she muttered, her gaze wandering to the barren walls.

Olivia's eyes widened as a realization sparked within her. "Wait," she exclaimed, her voice filled with a glimmer of hope. "My broom! It's spiritually connected to me. If I can muster enough energy, I might be able to perform a 'come to me' spell. The broom could find its way to us!"

Excitement mingled with skepticism in Benjamin's expression, yet he couldn't deny the slim possibility that lay before them. "It's worth a try," he said, his voice laced with cautious optimism. "We need every advantage we can get."

With the trio's consent, Olivia closed her eyes, channeling her inner strength. She focused on the connection she shared with her broom, envisioning it flying through the night sky, seeking a path to their confinement. Words of ancient power danced on her lips as she unleashed the incantation, sending her plea into the unknown.

Minutes passed, each heartbeat echoing with anticipation. Suddenly, a glimmer of moonlight danced upon the damp cellar walls. Olivia's eyes shot open in awe as her broom, slender and elegant, glided through the narrow bars of the window, defying the limitations of physicality.

A collective gasp escaped their lips, mingling awe with relief. Olivia's plan had worked, granting them a glimmer of hope amidst their dire circumstances.

"We have a way out," Olivia whispered, her voice filled with determination. "The broom may be our ticket to freedom."

Olivia's eyes widened with a mixture of astonishment and gratitude as she clutched the broom tightly in her hands. Her gaze fell upon the cloth bag attached to the broom, and her curiosity compelled her to unravel its contents. Carefully, she untied the drawstring, revealing a book adorned with familiar markings and the unmistakable aura of her mother's presence.

With the broom tightly held in Olivia's hands, she couldn't contain her excitement. Looking at Sophia and Benjamin, her eyes sparkled with anticipation. "This is incredible! It seems my mom and dad sensed we were in danger and ingeniously tied my book of shadows to the broom. That's how it found its way to us!"

Sophia and Benjamin exchanged astonished glances, marveling at the depth of Olivia's parents' love and foresight. "That's amazing," Sophia remarked, her voice filled with admiration. "Your parents knew we'd call for the broom, and they sent this book to help us escape. They must have known we needed a way out."

Olivia nodded, her heart brimming with gratitude. "Exactly. It's like they were watching over us, knowing we'd need a powerful spell to break free from Cassandra and the coven's clutches."

Benjamin's eyes glimmered with gratitude. "Your mom's book is our ticket to freedom. What's the spell called? How does it work?"

Olivia turned the pages until she found the carefully marked section. "It's called 'The Great Escape,'" she replied, her finger tracing the ancient text. "This spell is specifically designed for situations like ours. By channeling our collective energy and focusing on our desire to be free, it should create a burst of magic that can melt away any confinement."

Sophia's excitement mirrored Olivia's. "Let's do it. We've come so far, and we can't let Cassandra win."

Olivia nodded, her determination unyielding. "Absolutely. But we must be careful and focused. The spell is potent, and we don't know what other dangers may await us."

The trio huddled together in the cell, the book open before them, their hands intertwined in solidarity. Bathed in the moon's gentle glow, they prepared to recite the incantation.

Olivia took a deep breath, her voice steady yet charged with anticipation. "By the power within us, by the strength we share, let our spirits break these bars and soar through the air."

Sophia's voice joined in, filled with unwavering conviction. "Through darkest night, we claim our might, with magic's touch, the bars take flight."

Benjamin's voice echoed, brimming with determination. "No longer confined, our spirits unbound, we escape this cell, our freedom found."

As they chanted the words together, a powerful energy started to surge, crackling in the air around them. The room seemed to respond to their unified will, trembling as the magic grew stronger.

Then, in a dazzling burst of brilliance, the bars on the window began to melt away like liquid metal. The cell's iron grip was released, allowing the trio to step into newfound freedom.

As they climbed out through the open window, Olivia looked back at the now-dissolved bars, a sense of triumph filling her heart. "We did it," she whispered, disbelief mingling with exhilaration.

Sophia beamed at her friends. "We're finally free!"

Benjamin grinned, his spirit soaring with liberation. "Nothing can hold us back now!"

Olivia shared a knowing look with her companions. "Thank you both for being here. I'm grateful to have you by my side."

Sophia playfully nudged Olivia. "You know we're

with you all the way. Now, let's focus on stopping Cassandra and saving Ravenswood."

Benjamin's eyes widened as he glanced around, his voice urgent. "What should we do now? We've got to get out of here fast!"

Olivia's gaze turned to the broom in her hands, a glimmer of determination in her eyes. "There's one way," she replied, motioning towards the magical artifact. The others looked at her, astonishment evident on their faces.

Sophia hesitated for a moment, her voice filled with a mix of excitement and uncertainty. "Are you suggesting we... fly on the broom?"

Olivia nodded, a determined smile on her lips. "Yes, exactly. There's plenty of room on the broom for all of us. Besides, what choice do we have? We need to make a quick escape."

As the three of them climbed onto the broom, their hearts raced with a combination of fear and exhilaration. Olivia held the broom tightly, channeling her connection to it. With a surge of magic, the broom lifted off the ground, carrying them into the night sky.

The wind rushed through their hair as they soared above Cassandra's mansion, leaving the darkened estate behind. Olivia steered the broom with confidence, navigating through the night, guided by her instincts.

Benjamin's grip tightened around the broom handle, a mixture of awe and disbelief evident on his face. "I can't believe we're actually flying on a broom. This is incredible!"

Sophia's laughter filled the air as she held on tightly, the exhilaration washing away the lingering fear. "I guess Hogwarts isn't the only place where you can ride a broomstick!"

Olivia grinned, her focus on their destination. "Hold on, everyone. We're heading straight for my house. We'll regroup there, plan our next move, and find a way to stop Cassandra once and for all."

Chapter Seven

Reunited and Revelations

T he exhausted teens made their way back to Olivia's house, their hearts racing with a mix of relief and apprehension. As they reached the front door, Olivia's parents, Richard and Emily, swung it open with wide smiles of joy and relief.

"Thank goodness you're safe!" Emily exclaimed, enveloping Olivia in a tight embrace. Richard joined in, his eyes filled with paternal concern. "We were so worried about all of you. I'm so happy that you're all right."

Emily, still holding Olivia, turned her attention to Sophia and Benjamin, her gaze filled with warmth. "It's good to see you both safe and sound.

Come inside, let's talk."

Sophia, feeling a mix of gratitude and guilt, replied, "Thank you, Mrs. Harper. I can't imagine what my parents must be feeling right now."

Emily smiled reassuringly, her voice filled with understanding. "I've already spoken to your parents, Sophia. I let them know that you were spending the night here."

Benjamin, his tension easing, nodded gratefully. "Thank you, Mrs. Harper. That really saved my skin. But how'd you know to call our parents?"

"I've always believed in keeping a close eye on Olivia's well-being and her friendships," Emily explained. "I wanted to ensure everyone's safety, so when you kids didn't answer my call last night, I knew something was off. It was a mother's intuition, I suppose."

Emily led them into the cozy living room, offering them seats and refreshments. Olivia took a deep breath and began recounting their harrowing ordeal. She described their encounter with Cassandra, the imprisonment in the basement, and their escape aided by the broom and Emily's book of shadows.

After hearing Olivia's detailed retelling of the

events at Cassandra's mansion, Richard listened intently and then offered his advice. "It's highly probable that Cassandra will come after us once she realizes you've escaped," he said, his tone serious. "We need to be prepared for her return. She won't give up easily, especially with the power of the Blood Moon drawing near. Stay vigilant, and let's devise a plan to protect ourselves and Ravenswood from her dark intentions."

Olivia's eyes flickered with determination as she nodded in agreement. "You're right, Dad. We can't let Cassandra endanger our town or anyone else. We have to stop her once and for all."

Sophia, her fiery spirit undeterred, chimed in, "Count me in! I won't let her hurt anyone else with her twisted magic."

Benjamin, though still in awe of the recent events, nodded resolutely. "I may not have any magical powers, but I'll do whatever it takes to protect my friends and our town."

Richard placed a reassuring hand on Olivia's shoulder. "We'll face Cassandra together, as a united front. But first, we need to gather more information about her and her coven. We should consult your mother's book of shadows. It might hold some clues or spells that can aid us."

Emily nodded, her eyes gleaming with determination. "I'll start researching immediately. We'll find a way to counter Cassandra's dark magic."

As the evening progressed, the Harper household became a hub of activity. Olivia's family and her loyal friends huddled together, poring over the ancient pages of Emily's book of shadows. They studied spells, incantations, and protective enchantments, determined to arm themselves against Cassandra's impending return.

In the midst of their preparations, Olivia's mind raced, contemplating the upcoming confrontation. She couldn't shake the feeling that everything was leading to a climactic battle between light and darkness. The fate of Ravenswood hung in the balance, and she was determined to ensure that light would prevail.

Richard's eyes widened with concern as he reached for the remote control, turning on the television. The news anchor's voice filled the room, reporting the latest developments in Ravenswood.

"In a shocking turn of events, three more individuals in Ravenswood have fallen into unexplainable comas," the news anchor announced, her tone laced with urgency. "Medical professionals are baffled by these sudden cases, with no clear understanding of the cause or how to revive the affected individuals."

Olivia's heart sank, her mind instantly connecting the dots. "Cassandra," she whispered, her voice filled with a mix of anger and determination. "She's using her dark magic to drain the life force of innocent people."

Sophia's eyes widened in realization, her voice trembling with a mix of fear and resolve. "We have to stop her, Olivia. We can't let her continue hurting innocent people."

Benjamin's jaw clenched as he nodded in agreement. "It's not just about us anymore."

Emily, her gaze fixed on the television screen, spoke with a determined tone. "We must find a way to reverse the effects and awaken those who have fallen into comas. We can't let Cassandra's sinister plan succeed."

"Hey Livv, I think I found something in the book of shadows." Sophia piped up.

"What is it Sophia?" Olivia asked.

Sophia passed the book to Olivia. "Look at this."

On the page was an ancient prophecy foretelling the arrival of three chosen ones who possessed the unique ability to break the curse that had plagued Ravenswood for centuries.

"The three shall rise when darkness looms,
Bound by fate, their spirits groomed.
Together they'll face the shadows' dread,
To break the curse, their steps be led.

Through trials untold, they'll find the way,
Unraveling secrets that hold the sway.
Their hearts aligned, their souls aflame,
In unity, they'll change the game.

A spark of hope, a blaze of might,
To free the town from endless night.
When Blood Moon casts its crimson hue,
The chosen ones shall see it through."

As the words of the prophecy echoed in their minds, the realization dawned upon them. Olivia, Sophia, and Benjamin were the ones destined to fulfill this ancient prophecy. The weight of this newfound knowledge settled upon their shoulders, knowing that the fate of Ravenswood rested on their actions.

Despite the immense responsibility, hope surged through their veins. They were not alone in this journey. Olivia's family, Sophia's fiery spirit, and Benjamin's resourcefulness had led them this far, and they knew they could count on each other.

With the prophecy as their guide, they began to decipher its cryptic clues. The old tome spoke of three ancient artifacts hidden across the town, imbued with powerful magic that could counter Cassandra's dark curse.

Excitement filled the air as Olivia, Sophia, and Benjamin pored over the pages of the ancient book of shadows. The prophecy had provided them with a new sense of purpose and direction. They were the chosen ones, entrusted with the task of breaking the curse that had plagued Ravenswood for centuries.

"The artifacts," Olivia whispered, her eyes sparkling with determination. "According to the prophecy, they hold the key to countering Cassandra's dark curse. We must find them."

Sophia nodded, her fiery spirit burning bright. "Let's start with the first clue. It says the first artifact lies where the earth and sky converge under the ancient oak."

Benjamin, ever resourceful, pulled out a map of Ravenswood. "I remember an old oak tree near the town square. There's a plaque that says it's the oldest oak in Ravenswood. Perhaps that's where we need to go."

With their destination set, the three friends

prepared for their next quest. They gathered their supplies, ensuring they had everything they would need on their journey. The weight of their responsibility only fueled their determination.

Chapter Eight

Artifacts and Riddles

Arriving at the town square, they found the ancient oak, its branches stretching towards the sky. They followed the clue from the prophecy, searching for the convergence of earth and sky.

Olivia, Sophia, and Benjamin stood before the towering Old Oak, its gnarled branches reaching out like skeletal fingers. They could feel the weight of destiny resting upon their shoulders as they gazed at the ancient tree, its bark weathered by time and secrets.

Sophia took a step closer, her eyes scanning the

tree's massive trunk. "But how do we know for sure? What if we're at the wrong tree?"

Benjamin furrowed his brow, deep in thought. "The prophecy mentioned that the hidden chamber would be revealed at the 'Old Oak of the Chosen.' Perhaps there's something that sets this tree apart from the others."

Olivia's gaze darted around, searching for any distinguishing feature. And then, she spotted it— a cluster of ancient markings etched into the bark, forming a pattern unique to this particular tree.

"Look!" Olivia exclaimed, pointing to the markings. "These symbols... they match the ones in the book of shadows. This is the Old Oak of the Chosen!"

Sophia's eyes widened in realization. "You're right! It all lines up. The markings, the prophecy... This is the place we've been seeking."

"This is it," Olivia whispered, her voice filled with a mix of anticipation and trepidation. "According to the prophecy, the entrance to the hidden chamber lies beneath this old oak."

Sophia took a step closer, her eyes scanning the tree's massive trunk. "But how do we find it? It's not like there's a sign saying 'Secret Entrance Here.'"

Benjamin chuckled, a glimmer of excitement in his eyes. "That would make things too easy, wouldn't it? But fear not, my friends. If the prophecy is to be believed, we simply need to trust in the magic that guides us."

"Let's not waste any more time," Benjamin urged. "We have to explore beneath this tree and discover the hidden chamber."

As if on cue, a soft breeze rustled through the leaves, as if whispering ancient secrets. Olivia's heart skipped a beat as she noticed a peculiar pattern in the gnarled roots at the base of the Old Oak. It was as if they formed a hidden symbol, a doorway to another realm.

"Look!" Olivia exclaimed, her finger tracing the intricate lines of the symbol. "This is it! The entrance is here, right beneath our feet."

Sophia's eyes widened in awe. "Incredible! But how do we open it?"

Benjamin stepped forward, his voice laced with determination. "I believe it requires more than physical force. It demands something deeper."

The three friends joined hands, their palms pressed against the ancient symbol etched into the bark. A surge of energy coursed through their intertwined fingers, and the ground beneath them trembled. The roots of the Old Oak began to shift, revealing a hidden stairwell leading down into darkness.

Olivia took the first steps as they descended the stairs into the hidden chamber beneath the Old Oak, a chill air wrapped around them, sending shivers down their spines. The walls, hewn from rough stone, seemed to breathe with an ancient energy. Soft whispers echoed through the air, carried by a gentle breeze that whispered secrets long forgotten. The flickering glow of torches adorned the walls, casting dancing shadows that played tricks on their eyes.

The chamber itself was a vast cavern, its ceiling reaching high above, obscured by a veil of darkness. Stalactites and stalagmites punctuated the space, their jagged forms adding an otherworldly beauty to the surroundings. Moss and lichen clung to the walls, lending an eerie luminescence to the chamber.

The air was heavy with the scent of damp earth and time. The sound of dripping water echoed in the distance, creating a symphony of echoes that reverberated through the chamber. They treaded cautiously on the worn stone floor, their footsteps blending with the hushed whispers and the faint drips of water, creating an ethereal symphony of their own.

As their eyes adjusted to the dim light, they saw a pedestal at the center of the chamber. Upon it rested an artifact of immense power and significance. It was the Stone of Lumina, a radiant gem glowing with a soft, ethereal light. Its surface shimmered with intricate patterns, as if infused with the very essence of magic. The stone pulsated with an energy that seemed to harmonize with the chamber itself, resonating with a gentle hum that grew stronger as they approached.

Though there were no explicit markings, the stone's aura, its radiant glow, and the way it seemed to emanate a sense of profound importance were unmistakable. It was as if the Stone of Lumina carried its own silent narrative, telling the tale of its origin and purpose to those who were attuned to its frequencies.

Olivia's eyes shimmered with awe as she reached out to grasp the pendant. "We've done it. We've found one of the artifacts."

Sophia and Benjamin smiled, their faces reflecting a mixture of relief and triumph. "One step closer," Sophia said, her voice brimming with determination.

Olivia carefully wrapped the Stone of Lumina

in a soft cloth, preserving its radiant energy. As they ascended from the mystical cavern beneath the Old Oak, the shifting tree roots sealed the entrance behind them. Seeking a moment of respite, the three friends found a park bench where they could contemplate their next move. Olivia and Sophia opened the book of shadows, their eyes fixed on the prophecy that held the clue to their next destination.

Olivia and Sophia's fingers traced the delicate pages of the book of shadows, searching for the next clue that would lead them to their next destination. Sophia's voice filled the air as she read aloud the cryptic words:

"Where waves caress the golden shore, in depths serene, the secret's core. Follow the current, swift and clear, to find the next, the water's sphere."

The three friends exchanged curious glances, their minds already racing with possibilities. Benjamin spoke up, his voice filled with intrigue, "Waves, golden shore, and currents... It sounds like we're headed towards a body of water. But which one?"

Olivia's eyes sparkled with a newfound determination. "We have several rivers and lakes nearby. We'll need to find a place where the water is swift and clear, a place that stands out as a meeting point of serenity and power."

Sophia's face lit up as a memory flashed in her mind. "I remember a secluded waterfall not far from here. It's a hidden gem, untouched by many. The water cascades down with incredible force, creating a captivating spectacle."

Benjamin's voice held a note of excitement. "That could be it! The waterfall fits the description perfectly. It's a place where the water's sphere, its essence, is in its purest form."

The three friends embarked on their nature trek, following Sophia's memory towards the secluded waterfall. The trail had a mix of soft ground and rocks, and sunlight filtered through the dense canopy above. The air smelled like wildflowers, and the distant sound of flowing water guided their way.

When they reached the clearing with the majestic waterfall, they couldn't help but be awestruck by its beauty.

Sophia couldn't resist a little playful banter with Benjamin. She smirked and said, "Gotta admit, your eyes are as captivating as this breathtaking waterfall."

Benjamin, caught off guard but enjoying the

flirty vibes, grinned and replied, "Well, your smile could outshine the sun, lighting up this whole place."

Olivia, amused by their exchange, chuckled softly. "Aww, you two are adorable," she said affectionately. "Love is definitely in the air, even during our quest."

Sophia and Benjamin blushed, but the playful energy continued between them. They exchanged shy glances before continuing their journey, their light-hearted flirtation adding an extra spark to the adventure. Olivia couldn't help but smile, grateful for their friendship and the way they brightened even the most challenging moments.

The waterfall tumbled down from a towering cliff, its cascading waters glistening like silver threads in the sunlight. The pool below sparkled with a deep turquoise hue, inviting and mysterious. Surrounding the water's edge were large rocks and boulders, some of which were etched with curious symbols and markings.

Benjamin's keen eye caught sight of the engravings, and his excitement was palpable. "Look at this!" he called out, drawing the attention of Olivia and Sophia. Sophia's admiration for Benjamin's observation skills was evident, and she couldn't help but smile, secretly impressed by his abilities. Benjamin's cheeks turned slightly pink, but his excitement outweighed his embarrassment.

Olivia stepped forward, her fingers delicately tracing the ancient markings etched into the stone. To their astonishment, the symbols responded to her touch, faintly glowing with an otherworldly radiance. The air around them seemed to shimmer, as if responding to the power awakened by Olivia's connection.

Suddenly, the majestic waterfall before them parted like a grand theater curtain, revealing a hidden passage concealed behind the cascading water. The once hidden path now beckoned them forward, its mystery and allure impossible to resist.

The trio stepped inside, their senses enveloped by mist and echoes. Droplets of water hung in the air, creating a gentle melody as they collided and splashed against the smooth stone walls. The narrow pathway meandered deeper into the labyrinth, lit only by soft, ethereal rays of light that filtered through cracks in the rock above.

Olivia's voice carried through the chamber, filled with wonder and anticipation. "Can you feel it? There's something extraordinary about this place. It's like being in a realm untouched by time."

Sophia nodded, her eyes sparkling with

excitement. "Absolutely! The air feels charged with ancient power. Let's stay focused and keep an eye out for any clues or signs."

Benjamin chimed in, his tone cautious. "Agreed, but let's also stick close together. This labyrinth could be treacherous, and I don't want anyone getting lost."

As they ventured further into the labyrinth, the chamber opened up, revealing a magnificent underground grotto. The sound of rushing water grew louder, echoing off the walls, as they approached a grand pool surrounded by glistening stalactites and stalagmites. The water danced with an otherworldly luminescence, casting an enchanting glow upon their faces.

Pointing towards the shimmering pool, Benjamin continued, "Look, there! I think that's the Water Sphere we're searching for. It's emitting a mesmerizing radiance. But let's not lose focus. Stay close, and let's search this area carefully for any symbols or clues."

Olivia nodded, appreciating Benjamin's cautionary words. "You're right, Benjamin. We'll stick together and keep our wits about us."

Suddenly, Sophia's foot unexpectedly met a stone that gave way beneath her weight. Panic and fear surged through her as the ground crumbled, and she found herself teetering on the edge of a treacherous hole.

In that moment of desperation, fear etched upon her face, Sophia's instinctive reflexes kicked in. She extended her arm, her fingers grasping onto Benjamin's ankle with a desperate strength. Hanging on to him, she looked up with wide eyes, silently pleading for help.

Reacting swiftly, Benjamin's instincts kicked in. Without a second thought, he lunged forward, managing to grab Sophia's hand just in time before she could plunge into the dark abyss below. "Hold on, Sophia! I've got you!" he exclaimed, his voice firm with determination.

Sophia clung onto Benjamin's ankle with all her strength, tears welling up in her eyes as she tried to steady herself. "Please, be careful! Don't let go!" she pleaded, her voice trembling with fear.

"I won't let go, I promise!" Benjamin reassured her, his grip unwavering as he sought to pull her to safety. Bracing himself against the wall, he used all his strength to lift her, inch by inch, away from the perilous void. Sophia's fingers clung tightly to his hand, her trust in him unwavering.

In a moment of triumph, Benjamin heaved

Sophia upward, their combined efforts defying the dangers that lurked below. Sophia's body emerged from the pit, and as her feet found solid ground, she collapsed into Benjamin's waiting arms. Tears streamed down her face, mingling with a mixture of relief and gratitude.

With trembling hands, she clung to Benjamin, wrapping her arms around him in a tight embrace, her voice filled with gratitude and emotion. "Thank you, Benjamin. Thank you for saving me. I don't know what I would've done without you."

"You're safe now, Sophia. I've got you," Benjamin whispered, his voice filled with sincerity and a touch of vulnerability. His face flushed with a mix of emotions, Benjamin gently stroked her back, offering reassurance. "I've got you. I'll always be here to keep you safe," he murmured softly, his heart pounding in his chest.

With Sophia safely in his arms, Benjamin steadied their breathing, their collective resolve strengthening. Their hearts beat in unison, their bond forged even stronger by this near-tragic encounter.

As the intensity of the moment subsided, Olivia approached them, her concern evident. "Are you both okay?" she asked, her voice laced with worry.

Sophia nodded, still clinging to Benjamin as if afraid to let go. "Yes, thanks to Benjamin," she replied, her voice still shaky.

Olivia smiled at Benjamin, her admiration evident. "You did great, Benjamin. Thank you for saving her," she said sincerely.

Benjamin blushed once more, a mix of humility and pride in his eyes. "We're a team, right? We look out for each other," he said, trying to downplay his heroic act.

United by their shared experience, the trio continued their journey, now more aware than ever of the dangers that lay ahead.

As the trio stood before the shimmering pool, Olivia's eyes were drawn to the mesmerizing beauty of the water sphere. It glowed with an ethereal light, its surface reflecting the play of colors like a swirling rainbow. A sense of awe and reverence filled her as she realized that this was the Water Sphere they had sought.

With determination in her eyes, Olivia extended her hand towards the water sphere. She could feel the cool mist emanating from it, and a faint whisper seemed to call her name from within. She took a deep breath, steadying herself, and slowly immersed her hand into the pool.

The moment her fingertips touched the surface of the water sphere, a surge of energy coursed through her. It felt as if the very essence of water flowed into her being, connecting her to the elemental power contained within. She closed her eyes, allowing the sensations to wash over her.

With a gentle pull, Olivia lifted the water sphere from the pool, cradling it in her hands. It radiated a soothing aura, and droplets of water cascaded from it, creating a soft melody as they hit the ground. Olivia felt a profound connection to the element of water, as if it acknowledged her as its guardian.

She turned towards Sophia and Benjamin, her eyes filled with a mixture of excitement and determination. "We've found it," she said, her voice filled with a newfound confidence. "The Water Sphere. This is one step closer to breaking the curse of Ravenswood."

Sophia and Benjamin looked at Olivia with awe and admiration. They could sense the immense power emanating from the water sphere and the newfound resolve in Olivia's words. They knew that their journey was far from over, but with each artifact they acquired, their bond grew stronger, and their purpose clearer.

Chapter Nine

Embers Of Faith

As they emerged from the labyrinth behind the waterfall, they found themselves bathed in the warm glow of sunlight. Olivia's heart raced with anticipation as she opened the Book of Shadows once again to find the final clue.

"Listen, I think I've found something," she said, her voice filled with excitement. "It says, 'Descend to the depths where faith burns bright, within the sacred halls where flames dance with eternal light.'"

Sophia's eyes widened with realization. "The depths of faith... Sacred halls... It must be hidden within a church," she pondered aloud, her voice filled with a sense of reverence.

Benjamin's gaze shifted, his mind racing with possibilities. "Wait, there's an old church on the outskirts of town, known for its ancient catacombs and hidden chambers," he suggested, his voice tinged with excitement. "Perhaps that's where we need to go."

Olivia nodded, a sense of purpose burning within her. "Yes, the church aligns with the clues. It's a place where faith burns bright, and the flames of devotion meet the eternal light," she affirmed.

So, the trio set their sights on the distant old Catholic church that Benjamin had mentioned. As they realized the considerable distance they would need to cover, Sophia's exasperation became evident. "There's no way we can possibly walk that far!" she exclaimed, her voice filled with disbelief.

Olivia nodded in agreement, realizing the practicality of Sophia's concern. "You're right. This is a job for my trusty broom," she declared, determination gleaming in her eyes. She paused for a moment, centering herself, and focused her energy on summoning the broom, just as she had done in the direst of moments before.

With each passing second, the air crackled with anticipation. And just as they had hoped, the familiar sight of Olivia's broom came swooping through the air, like a loyal companion answering her call. It glided gracefully into Olivia's outstretched hands, its bristles brimming with energy.

Sophia's eyes widened in awe, marveling at the enchanted object before them. "That's amazing, Olivia! You really have a way with that broom," she exclaimed, her admiration evident.

Olivia smiled, a mix of pride and gratitude shining in her eyes. "Thanks, Sophia." She patted the broom affectionately before turning to Benjamin. "Hop on, guys! We've got a church to reach."

With eager anticipation, Sophia and Benjamin climbed onto the broom, making themselves comfortable behind Olivia. Gripping tightly to the broom's handle, Olivia felt the rush of magical energy course through her as she willed it to lift off the ground. The broom obeyed her command, ascending smoothly into the air.

As they soared above the treetops, the wind whipped through their hair, and the world beneath them shrank into miniature. The journey to the old Catholic church was swift and thrilling, a testament to Olivia's mastery of her magical steed. They marveled at the breathtaking view of Ravenswood stretched out below them, a town steeped in history and mystery.

Soon, the spires of the ancient church came into view, rising like guardian sentinels against the sky. Olivia skillfully maneuvered the broom, guiding it down to a gentle landing in the churchyard. The teens dismounted, their hearts still racing from the exhilarating flight.

They approached the massive wooden doors of the church, pushing them open with a creak. The scent of polished wood and ancient stone filled the air, adding to the sacred atmosphere that enveloped the place. They stepped inside, their footsteps echoing softly in the cavernous space.

As they ventured deeper into the church, they admired the beautiful stained-glass windows depicting stories of faith and devotion. The flickering candlelight created an ethereal glow, casting dancing shadows upon the hallowed walls.

The trio explored every nook and cranny of the old church, searching for clues that might guide them to the location of the Fire Ember. They inspected religious relics, old scriptures, and sacred artworks with keen eyes, hoping to uncover the next piece of the puzzle.

As Olivia's gaze shifted towards the majestic statue in the heart of the church, she couldn't shake the feeling that it held a crucial clue for their quest. It stood tall and imposing, with an outstretched arm pointing resolutely towards the left, as if beckoning them to follow its guidance.

Her voice laced with excitement and determination, Olivia shared her insight with Sophia and Benjamin. "Look, the statue seems to be pointing in a specific direction. Maybe it's trying to show us the way to the Fire Ember."

Sophia's eyes widened as she absorbed Olivia's observation. "You might be onto something, Livv."

Benjamin nodded, his curiosity piqued. "It's worth a shot. Plus, we've come this far. No harm in exploring further."

They ventured deeper into the dimly lit corridors of the church, their footsteps echoing off the ancient stone walls. With each turn they took, the atmosphere grew more charged with anticipation. Olivia's heart raced with a mix of excitement and a touch of trepidation. She couldn't help but wonder what awaited them at the end of this path.

The trio moved in unison, venturing deeper into the old church. They came across a section of the wall that appeared slightly different from the rest, subtly hinting at a concealed passage.

In that moment, as if by some serendipitous accident, a hidden mechanism within the wall was triggered.

With a creak and a low rumble, the stone floor beneath their feet shifted, revealing a concealed passageway that led into the depths of the catacombs. The trio exchanged startled glances, their hearts pounding with a mixture of surprise and anticipation.

"That... that wasn't us," Benjamin stuttered, his eyes widening.

Olivia's voice trembled with a mixture of excitement and uncertainty. "It seems the statue... the church itself, is guiding us."

Sophia's curiosity ignited, overshadowing any fear. "Well, what are we waiting for? Let's see where it leads us!"

With cautious steps, they entered the secret passageway, guided by the dim glow of torches that lined the stone walls. The air grew cooler as they descended deeper into the catacombs, their senses heightened by the eerie ambiance surrounding them.

Sophia couldn't help but let out a sarcastic

remark amidst the awe and excitement.

"Wow, another hidden chamber? Whoever hid these artifacts must have been a real fan of creepy surprises, it's like they couldn't resist the urge to make it as mysterious and dramatic as possible. Secret passages, catacombs, hidden chambers... they really went all out."

Benjamin grinned, shaking his head. "I guess they wanted to keep things interesting for anyone brave enough to seek these artifacts. Can't blame them for having a flair for the dramatic."

Sophia playfully rolled her eyes. "Well, they definitely succeeded. If I ever need to hide something important, I'll be sure to stash it away in an ancient crypt guarded by puzzles and riddles. That's foolproof!"

The winding corridors seemed to stretch endlessly, revealing glimpses of crypts and ancient symbols etched into the walls. The flickering torchlight cast long, dancing shadows that seemed to whisper secrets of the past.

"Stay close," Benjamin advised, his voice laced with concern. "These catacombs can be treacherous, and we don't want a repeat of earlier."

Sophia blushed slightly.

As they ventured deeper into the catacombs, the darkness seemed to engulf them, amplifying the mystery and anticipation that filled the air. Their footsteps echoed through the silent corridors, accompanied by occasional scurrying from unseen sources.

Sophia's voice broke the silence. "This place is both haunting and awe-inspiring. Just imagine the stories these walls could tell."

Finally, they arrived at a chamber adorned with intricate carvings and adorned with symbols of fire.

As Olivia, Sophia, and Benjamin cautiously stepped into the room that housed the Fire Ember, a faint whisper filled the air. It was a voice, soft and ethereal, calling out Olivia's name. She paused, her eyes widening in surprise as she glanced around to see if her friends had heard it too. But Sophia and Benjamin looked at her curiously, unaware of the mysterious voice that resonated only with her.

"Did you guys hear that?" Olivia asked, her voice tinged with a mix of excitement and apprehension.

Sophia and Benjamin exchanged puzzled glances, shaking their heads in response. "Hear what?" Sophia asked.

Olivia's gaze returned to the gleaming Fire Ember, its fiery glow captivating her attention. She took a tentative step forward, the artifact seemingly drawing her closer. Once again, the voice whispered, this time louder and more distinct, resonating within her mind.

"Olivia... Olivia..."

Her heart raced with a mix of anticipation and curiosity. It was as if the Fire Ember had recognized her, calling out to her in a way that defied explanation. Determined to uncover the truth, Olivia leaned closer to the artifact, her voice barely above a whisper.

"Who... Who are you?" she asked, her words barely escaping her lips.

The room fell silent, the whispering voice fading away. Olivia was left with a sense of wonder, a connection forged between her and the ancient artifact. She knew that the Fire Ember held secrets, and she was determined to unlock them, to understand the significance of its call to her.

As Olivia carefully secured the Fire Ember with the other collected artifacts, a sense of urgency coursed through her. She turned to her friends with determination in her eyes, realizing that they needed to make their way back to her house swiftly. She knew that the answers they sought, the key to breaking the curse, lay within the pages of the Book of Shadows.

"Come on, we can't waste any more time," Olivia urged, her voice filled with a mix of excitement and concern. "We have to get back to my house and consult the Book of Shadows. It holds the next steps to break the curse."

Sophia and Benjamin nodded in agreement, their hearts racing with anticipation. They knew the stakes were high, and their encounter with Cassandra had only reinforced the urgency of their mission. Together, they moved quickly through the catacombs, retracing their steps, and emerging back into the dimly lit church.

However, as they approached the exit, their excitement was abruptly shattered by an unexpected sight. Standing before them, an insidious smirk gracing her face, was Cassandra herself. In her clutches, she held Olivia's precious broom.

Olivia's heart sank, a mix of anger and fear gripping her. "Cassandra, what do you want?" she demanded, her voice trembling with a fierce determination.

Cassandra's cold laughter echoed through the churchyard, sending shivers down their spines. "Oh, my dear Olivia, you thought you could escape me so easily? Your little flying toy won't save you now. Hand over the artifacts, and perhaps I'll consider sparing your friends."

Sophia clenched her fists, her eyes narrowing in defiance. "You won't get away with this, Cassandra. We're stronger together, and we won't let you win."

Benjamin, though shaken by the unexpected confrontation, stood tall. "Give us back the broom, Cassandra. We won't let you stand in our way."

Their words hung in the air, a challenge thrown at the feet of their nemesis. The trio braced themselves, ready to face whatever Cassandra had planned. Their determination burned brighter than ever as they prepared to confront the darkness that threatened to consume their town and their lives.

Chapter Ten

The Night of the Blood Moon

Cassandra's triumphant laughter filled the air as she effortlessly restrained Olivia, Sophia, and Benjamin with her dark magic. The chains wrapped around them, their glow matching the ominous aura of the blood moon above. With a wave of her hand, she transported them to her foreboding mansion, the embodiment of her twisted desires.

The grand doors of the mansion swung open, revealing a dimly lit foyer adorned with haunting portraits and flickering candles. Cassandra, wearing a sinister grin, led them through the echoing halls, each step resonating with an air of impending doom.

Cassandra led Olivia, Sophia, and Benjamin into a grand room, illuminated by dim torchlight. The flickering flames danced ominously, casting eerie shadows on the stone walls. In the center of the room, a lavish throne stood, adorned with intricate carvings, as if a symbol of Cassandra's twisted self-proclaimed royalty.

As the trio took in the sight before them, their hearts sank with a mix of disbelief and dread. There, in chains, stood Olivia's parents, Richard and Emily, their faces etched with worry and fear. Olivia's voice trembled as she called out to them in astonishment.

"Mom! Dad! How... How did this happen?" Olivia's voice quivered with a mixture of shock and concern.

Cassandra's wicked laughter filled the room, echoing off the walls like a haunting melody. She strutted towards the throne, taking her place with an air of smug superiority. Her eyes gleamed with malevolence as she scoffed at Olivia's astonishment.

"Did you really think I would overlook the opportunity to capture your dear parents, Olivia?" Cassandra sneered. "Oh, how easily they fell into my clutches. Your mother's pleading eyes and your father's futile attempts to resist—it was all quite entertaining."

Olivia's hands clenched into fists, her determination ignited by the sight of her captive parents. She exchanged a determined glance with Sophia and Benjamin, silently reaffirming their shared resolve to save Olivia's family and put an end to Cassandra's reign of darkness.

With a wicked smile stretching across her face, Cassandra relished in revealing the reason behind her scheme to amplify the curse's power. Her voice dripped with a venomous satisfaction as she addressed Olivia, her words laced with cruelty.

"Welcome, dear Olivia, to my court," Cassandra sneered, her eyes glinting with malicious intent. "You may be wondering why I went to such great lengths to capture your parents and lure you all into my grasp. Well, let me enlighten you."

Olivia's heart raced, a mix of fear and anger coursing through her veins. She braced herself for Cassandra's revelation, knowing it would be nothing short of twisted.

"You see, my dear, I am not merely an ordinary witch," Cassandra continued, her voice dripping with self-assured arrogance. "I am a direct descendant of the powerful witch Seraphina herself, the very one who cast the curse upon your...

our... wretched bloodline. It runs in our blood, this darkness that taints our souls."

A mixture of shock and disbelief flickered across Olivia's face, but Cassandra paid no mind. She reveled in the chaos she had unleashed.

"The curse has plagued this town for generations, and now it is time for it to reach its pinnacle," Cassandra declared, her voice growing more commanding. "By sacrificing you, dear Olivia, I will not only avenge Seraphina's legacy, but I will ensure my own survival. With your blood spilled, the curse's hold on me will be broken, and I will rise as the true queen of The Ravenswood Witches."

Olivia's mind raced, her thoughts a whirlwind of emotions and defiance. She refused to let Cassandra's claims define her or her family's fate. Summoning her courage, she met Cassandra's gaze with unwavering determination.

"You may believe that your twisted lineage gives you power, Cassandra, but true strength lies in the bonds we share," Olivia retorted, her voice laced with defiance. "Love, unity, and resilience are forces far greater than any curse you can conjure. We will stand against your darkness, united and unwavering."

Cassandra's laughter echoed through the

chamber, an unsettling sound that chilled the air. She relished in the teens' defiance, finding amusement in their futile attempts to challenge her authority.

"How amusing it is to witness such naive bravery," Cassandra scoffed, her voice laced with contempt. "You think your words hold any weight against the might of the curse? You are but mere pawns in the grand tapestry of fate, my dear. Your resistance is futile, and your unity will crumble before the might of my power."

Olivia's resolve hardened, her voice cutting through Cassandra's mockery. "We may be pawns, but we are pawns with free will," she declared, her words ringing with unwavering determination. "And we choose to defy you, Cassandra. We choose to fight for the light, for love, and for the liberation of Ravenswood from your twisted grasp."

Cassandra's laughter subsided, replaced by a dangerous glint in her eyes. She was not accustomed to being defied, especially by those she deemed inferior. The teens' boldness only fueled her desire to break them.

"You think your feeble attempts at resistance will alter the course of fate?" Cassandra sneered. "I will relish watching your hopes crumble and your precious unity shatter. Prepare yourselves for the impending darkness, for it will consume you all!"

Cassandra called for the elemental artifacts to be brought to her. One of her coven brought them and they were laid out. The Stone of Lumina, the Water Sphere, and the Fire Ember. Cassandra explained that these artifacts could not only break the curse but, if used for evil, could make it even stronger.

"Behold, the very keys to your salvation or your demise," Cassandra proclaimed, her voice carrying an ominous weight. "These artifacts have the potential to break the curse that has haunted our lineage for centuries. Yet, they are also conduits of immense power, capable of magnifying the darkness that courses through Ravenswood."

Olivia's eyes flickered between the artifacts, a mixture of awe and trepidation filling her heart. She couldn't help but be captivated by their beauty, even as the weight of their potential consequences weighed heavily on her mind.

Cassandra's lips curled into a wicked smile as she continued her taunting discourse. "With the Stone of Lumina, the light of hope and purity, the curse could be banished forever. The Water Sphere, a vessel of ancient wisdom and healing, could wash away the darkness that plagued us. And the Fire Ember, a symbol of passion and strength, could ignite the flames of liberation."

She paused for a moment, relishing in the apprehension etched upon the faces of the captives. "But, my dear Olivia, imagine the power we could wield if we harnessed these artifacts for darker purposes," Cassandra whispered, her voice dripping with temptation. "With them, we could enshroud Ravenswood in an even greater shroud of darkness. We could command the very forces that have tormented us, bending them to our will."

Olivia's heart pounded in her chest as she stared at the artifacts, their allure and potential danger captivating her thoughts. She knew the consequences of such power falling into the wrong hands, and she could feel the weight of her choice pressing upon her.

"No," Olivia's voice trembled, but her resolve remained unyielding. "I will not allow these artifacts to be used for evil, to perpetuate the curse that has plagued us for far too long. We must break free from its grasp, not succumb to its allure."

Cassandra's laughter echoed through the chamber, a chilling sound that sent shivers down their spines. "Oh, my dear Olivia, how your naivety blinds you," she sneered. "You speak of breaking free, yet you fail to see the true power that lies within these artifacts. Their potential for darkness far outweighs any feeble attempts at liberation."

Olivia's parents exchanged worried glances, their hearts aching for their daughter's plight. They knew the danger that Cassandra's covetousness posed to their family and the town. With a shared resolve, they offered words of encouragement to Olivia, reminding her of the strength and goodness that resided within her.

The battle for the artifacts had begun, not only against the physical restraints that held them captive but against the darkness that threatened to consume their world. The outcome would hinge on the choices they made and the strength of their unity against the allure of power.

Cassandra's eyes gleamed with a sinister light as Olivia stood firm in her resolve. The defiance only seemed to fuel her determination. With a wicked smile, she dismissed Olivia's words as mere trivialities.

"Foolish girl, do you truly believe your feeble resistance can thwart me?" Cassandra taunted, her voice dripping with venomous arrogance. "You have no idea of the power I command, the depths of darkness that reside within me. These artifacts will be the instruments of your demise."

She raised her hands, her fingers entwined in

an intricate dance of malevolence. The air crackled with an ominous energy as the room became suffused with a malignant aura. Shadows danced along the walls, their eerie forms undulating with Cassandra's every movement.

"By the blood moon's light, by the ancient incantations passed down through generations, I invoke the powers that have slumbered for far too long," Cassandra chanted, her voice resonating with an otherworldly echo. "May the forces of darkness heed my call, may their malevolence be unleashed upon this cursed land."

Olivia's heart raced with a mixture of fear and determination. She couldn't let Cassandra succeed, couldn't allow her plans of destruction to come to fruition. With a steely resolve, she glanced at Benjamin and Sophia, silently communicating their shared purpose.

"We won't let you succeed, Cassandra," Olivia retorted, her voice quivering with a newfound strength. "The power of unity and love will always prevail over darkness and hatred."

Cassandra's laughter echoed through the chamber, a cacophony of derision. "Love? Unity? Such feeble sentiments, my dear," she sneered. "Your misplaced faith in such trivialities is nothing but a testament to your own foolishness."

The room seemed to pulse with an ominous energy as Cassandra's incantation reached its crescendo. The air crackled with anticipation, and the artifacts on the table trembled as if responding to the call of their malevolent mistress.

Olivia's gaze flickered between the artifacts and her parents, their eyes filled with a mixture of fear and hope. She knew that the time for action was now, that they couldn't afford to stand idly by while darkness consumed their world.

"Stand strong, everyone!" Olivia's voice rang out, her words carrying a resolute determination. "We may be chained, but our spirits are free. Together, we can overcome any darkness that threatens to engulf us."

Cassandra's eyes narrowed, her anger flaring at Olivia's defiance. "You dare to challenge me? To believe in such trivial notions of hope and unity?" she spat. "I will show you the true depths of despair, the futility of your resistance."

The room seemed to tremble as Cassandra's incantation reached its zenith. Shadows coiled and writhed like serpents, engulfing the chamber in an impenetrable darkness. The air grew heavy with malevolence, suffocating all hope in its wake.

But even in the face of overwhelming darkness, Olivia refused to yield. With a fierce determination burning in her eyes, she locked gazes with Cassandra, ready to face whatever darkness lay ahead.

The battle between light and darkness had begun, and the outcome hinged on the strength of their wills, the power of love, and the belief in a better future.

Suddenly, a cloaked figure burst into the room, wielding a wand with a resolute grip. The air crackled with anticipation as the figure unleashed a powerful blast of energy, propelling Cassandra backward, her body crashing against the unforgiving wall.

Cassandra, seething with anger and defiance, retaliated by flinging her hands in a desperate attempt to regain control. But the figure remained resilient, weathering the assault and readying themselves for the next move.

As Cassandra struggled to regain her footing, the hood of the figure's cloak slipped away, revealing the young woman who had shown kindness by bringing food to the imprisoned teens. Her eyes burned with a fierce resolve as she confronted Cassandra, her wand held firmly in her grasp.

Her eyes burned with determination as she pointed the wand towards Cassandra once more. Another surge of energy erupted from its tip, striking Cassandra with a force that sent her sprawling to the ground.

With the immediate threat subdued, the young woman shifted her focus to Olivia and her captive parents. Understanding the urgency of the situation, she channeled her magic towards their chains, casting a vibrant red light that danced along the links. The chains shattered into pieces, setting the captives free.

"Go! Quickly, gather the elements and get out of here!" the young woman called out, her voice filled with urgency. "I'll hold Cassandra off. Make haste!"

Olivia hesitated for a moment, torn between the urgency to escape and her desire to help the young woman. But the determination in the young woman's eyes convinced her that she had to trust in this unexpected ally.

With a nod of understanding, Olivia motioned for Benjamin, Sophia, and her parents to follow her lead. They dashed towards the table where the elemental artifacts lay, scooping them up and clutching them tightly in their hands. Olivia grabbed her broom and the Book Of Shadows as she ran toward the exit.

Meanwhile, the young woman faced Cassandra, who had risen to her feet, fury evident in her every move. The room crackled with the intensity of their confrontation as they squared off, each holding their ground.

"You can't stop me, interloper!" Cassandra spat, her voice seething with rage. "These artifacts will be mine, and the curse will be unbreakable!"

The young woman's voice rang out with a strength that belied her appearance. "You underestimate the power of hope and the strength of those who stand together against darkness," she retorted defiantly.

With renewed determination, the young woman thrust her wand forward, and a burst of energy shot forth, engaging Cassandra in a magical battle that danced with dazzling lights and shadowy tendrils. The air was charged with an otherworldly energy as they clashed, each one seeking to gain the upper hand.

Olivia, Benjamin, Sophia, and Olivia's parents reached the doorway, their hearts pounding with a mixture of fear and hope. Olivia glanced back one last time at the young woman, who was bravely standing against the malevolent force of Cassandra.

"We won't forget you!" Olivia called out, her voice filled with gratitude and admiration.

The young woman smiled warmly amidst the chaos of the battle. "Just go," she replied. "Your destiny awaits, and I'll make sure Cassandra won't trouble you any longer."

With that assurance, the teens and Olivia's parents hurriedly made their escape from the mansion, clutching the elemental artifacts tightly to their chests. As they raced through the darkened corridors and into the night, they knew that they had a newfound ally in the young woman, someone willing to risk everything to help them break the curse.

Chapter Eleven

Uniting The Elements

The night of the blood moon hung ominously over the land as Olivia and her family raced back to their house. The weight of urgency pressed upon them, knowing that Cassandra could still be in pursuit, her desire for power stronger than ever. They needed to break the curse before she could enact her malevolent plans.

In the kitchen, the artifacts and the Book of Shadows were laid out on the table. The elemental artifacts—the Stone of Lumina, the Water Sphere, and the Fire Ember—gleamed in the moonlight, their power evident to all who beheld them. Olivia's hands trembled with a mix of anxiety and hope as she flipped through the pages of the ancient book, searching for the incantation that could unite the elements and break the curse.

"Found it!" Olivia exclaimed, her voice tinged with excitement and determination. "This is the incantation that will bring all the elements together. We must repeat it three times, with unwavering conviction."

Olivia's family, Benjamin, and Sophia gathered around the table, their hands clasped together, forming a tight circle. The room seemed to hum with the energy of the artifacts and the power of the blood moon. Olivia cleared her throat, her voice strong and unwavering as she began to recite the incantation.

"By the power of earth, water, and fire, we unite. From ancient realms, our spirits take flight. Break the chains that hold us tight, undo the curse with this sacred rite."

Together, they chanted the incantation, their voices harmonizing as they called upon the forces of the elements to aid them in their quest. The artifacts seemed to pulse with energy, resonating with the power of the incantation. Each time they repeated the words, the room filled with a soft glow, illuminating their determined faces.

"By the power of earth, water, and fire, we unite. From ancient realms, our spirits take flight. Break the chains that hold us tight, undo the curse with this sacred rite."

Olivia's heart pounded in her chest as they reached the final repetition, their voices growing stronger and more resolute with each iteration.

"By the power of earth, water, and fire, we unite. From ancient realms, our spirits take flight. Break the chains that hold us tight, undo the curse with this sacred rite."

As the last words left their lips, a brilliant surge of light burst from the artifacts, swirling and intertwining in a dance of mystic energy. The room seemed to vibrate with the force of the united elements. For a moment, time stood still, and the world seemed to hold its breath.

And then, just as suddenly as it had begun, the light receded, and a profound stillness settled over the room. Olivia looked around, her heart pounding with hope and trepidation. Had it worked?

A soft, radiant glow enveloped each artifact, signifying their transformation into something more than mere objects. The curse that had plagued Olivia's family for generations seemed to unravel, the weight that had burdened their souls lifting away.

"We did it!" Olivia's father exclaimed, his voice filled with joy and wonder.

The family embraced, their tears of relief mingling with the newfound hope that enveloped them. Benjamin and Sophia grinned from ear to ear, knowing they had played a significant part in this extraordinary moment.

Outside, the blood moon slowly began to wane, its malevolent influence dissipating as the curse was broken. The darkness that had threatened to consume them now gave way to the dawn of a new day, filled with possibilities and freedom.

In the afterglow of their victory, Olivia couldn't help but think of the young woman who had bravely confronted Cassandra, risking everything to ensure their escape. She hoped that their unexpected ally had emerged triumphant and that they would meet again, their paths forever intertwined.

After the intense culmination of their journey, Olivia, Sophia, and Benjamin sought solace and respite on the porch, allowing the weight of their adventures to slowly lift from their shoulders. Sophia and Benjamin found comfort in each other's presence, their bodies swaying gently on the porch swing, a subtle reflection of the harmony they had discovered amidst chaos.

Sophia leaned her head against Benjamin's shoulder, a soft smile playing on her lips. "You know," she said, her voice filled with a mix of exhaustion and contentment, "I never imagined we'd go through something like this together."

Benjamin nodded, his gaze fixed on the horizon as if lost in thought. "Yeah, it's been quite the journey," he replied, his voice tinged with a sense of wonder. "Who would've thought we'd uncover hidden chambers, face booby traps, and battle ancient curses?"

Olivia joined them on the swing, the porch bathed in the soft glow of the rising sun. She took a deep breath, savoring the stillness of the moment. "It's hard to believe everything we've experienced," she admitted, her eyes filled with gratitude. "But we did it. Against all odds, we triumphed."

Sophia looked at Olivia, a glimmer of awe in her eyes. "You were the heart and soul of our team, Olivia," she said, her voice filled with admiration. "Your unwavering belief in us, your leadership—it's what carried us through."

Benjamin interjected, a playful smile crossing his face. "And let's not forget your knack for finding hidden clues and deciphering ancient riddles," he teased, earning a playful shove from Sophia.

Olivia laughed, a sound that echoed with the joy of their shared victory. "We all had our strengths," she said, her voice tinged with humility. "But it was our friendship, our unwavering support for each other, that truly made us unstoppable."

As they sat there, the porch enveloped in a comfortable silence, the faint sound of a news report drifted out from the open door. The anchor's voice carried hope as they announced the awakening of the coma patients, a tangible sign that their actions had not been in vain.

The trio exchanged glances, their faces alight with a renewed sense of purpose. "We did more than break a curse," Olivia said, her voice filled with a mix of pride and determination. "We brought hope, healing, and a second chance to those who needed it most."

Sophia nodded, a sense of fulfillment shining in her eyes. "And we'll carry that spirit with us," she affirmed, her voice resolute. "In every challenge we face, we'll remember what we're capable of—what we achieved together."

Benjamin leaned back, his gaze fixed on the horizon, his voice carrying a note of quiet confidence. "The world is full of mysteries, adventures waiting to be discovered," he mused. "And we'll be ready for whatever comes our way, knowing that as long as we have each other, we can overcome anything."

As the sun's gentle rays illuminated their faces, the three friends sat together on the porch, cherishing the bonds they had forged and the victories they had achieved, forever bound by the extraordinary journey they had shared. And as they embraced the dawn of a new day, they carried within them the lessons learned, the friendships strengthened, and a sense of endless possibility.

Epilogue

The events that had unfolded during their fateful journey had forever changed the lives of Olivia, Sophia, and Benjamin. As they stood together, gazing out at the horizon, they marveled at the world that lay before them, brimming with untold adventures and mysteries waiting to be unraveled.

Their bond remained unbreakable, and their hearts were filled with the echoes of their shared triumphs and the laughter they had shared along the way. The curse had been broken, and the Shadowsong family had finally found peace. The darkness that had once shrouded their lives had been replaced by a renewed sense of hope and possibility.

But little did they know, their journey was far from

over. Deep within the realm of magic, a new threat was brewing, one that would test their newfound strength and challenge everything they thought they knew. The whispers of a forgotten prophecy reached their ears, hinting at a power far greater than they had ever encountered.

As they contemplated the next steps of their lives, a mysterious letter arrived, bearing an emblem they recognized from their past adventures. The ink on the parchment shimmered with an ethereal glow, urging them to embark on a new quest—one that would lead them to the heart of a hidden world, teeming with ancient secrets and powerful artifacts.

With hearts full of anticipation and a burning curiosity, they gathered once again, their hands clasped tightly together, ready to face the unknown. They knew that this new journey would test their courage, friendship, and the very essence of who they were. The echoes of their previous triumphs fueled their determination, reminding them that they were capable of overcoming any challenge that lay ahead.

As they set off on their new adventure, the possibilities seemed endless. They were no longer ordinary teenagers, but heroes with destinies intertwined with the magic that pulsed through their veins. The world awaited their next chapter, eager to witness the extraordinary feats they were destined to achieve.

And so, as they embarked on this new quest, their hearts filled with hope, their souls ablaze with anticipation, and their minds ready to unravel the mysteries that lay in wait, they knew that their journey was far from over. The sequel to their tale was about to unfold, and they were ready to write the next chapter of their extraordinary story.

The end... for now.

Made in the USA
Middletown, DE
09 July 2023